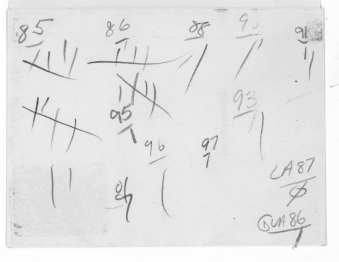

THE HALFHYDE LINE

THE HALFHYDE LINE

Philip McCutchan

St. Martin's Press
New York

7-85 BT 1095

Library of Congress Cataloging in Publication Data

McCutchan, Philip, 1920-
    The Halfhyde line.

    I. Title.
PR6063.A167H32   1985   823'.914   84-22868
ISBN 0-312-35686-2

First published in Great Britain by George Weidenfeld & Nicolson Ltd.

First U.S. Edition

10 9 8 7 6 5 4 3 2 1

THE HALFHYDE LINE

ONE

'It's a fine harbour,' Halfhyde said.

His companion gave him a scathing glance. 'Best in the world. Captain Cook, he may have been a bloody pommie, but he knew a thing or two. When he found Port Jackson, he reckoned it was pretty good. So do I. Just look at it.'

Halfhyde did; not for the first time, though his entry between Sydney Heads in the old windjammer *Aysgarth Falls* under Captain McRafferty had been his first experience of Australian waters. That had been some months earlier and in the meantime he had been busy looking for a ship with which to found his own line. Now, in company with William Sturt, a director of the Australian Joint Stock Bank, he was looking down on Port Jackson from the lawns of Government House – overlooking Farm Cove and surrounded by the Domain and the Botanic Gardens. It was a splendid morning, one of sun and sparkle with a light breeze ruffling the blue waters of the harbour as they washed the shores of Sydney Town, a fine morning on which to do business and found a shipping line. Such was now within Halfhyde's grasp and he was glad when Sturt turned from the prospect of beauty spread below him and got down to brass tacks.

'I understand you have the money through,' Sturt said.

'I have.' The draft had arrived three days earlier by the mail steamer from Tilbury: thirty thousand pounds sterling from his wife's Uncle Henry. At the same time a letter had come, also from Henry Willard, congratulating him on having found a ship to suit him. Halfhyde had read the letter with affection: his father-in-law's brother, unlike his father-in-law, had been a good friend who understood well enough how Halfhyde had been inveigled into matrimony – with Miss Mildred Willard as was, only and plain daughter of Halfhyde's former senior officer, Vice-Admiral Sir John Willard. Halfhyde, now no longer even a half-pay lieutenant of the Royal Navy, was, it seemed, totally out of Sir John's regard, as totally as he was out of the Queen's service. Mildred, according to Uncle Henry, was still indulging in an extended attack of the vapours. Even the dread word divorce had been uttered in the Willard home in the High Street of Old Portsmouth . . . though Uncle Henry believed it would not come to that when his brother came face to face with the certainty of scandal, the ostracism of his family from decent society, and the equal certainty that no-one else would marry his daughter. Mildred, the cross that Lady Willard had been determined to shift on to Halfhyde's shoulders, would remain firmly about those of Sir John. Halfhyde felt no remorse; Mildred had been a disaster from the moment she had turned in horror from all matrimonial advances on the first night of the honeymoon. Uncle Henry had been his deliverance, suggesting that Halfhyde should go back to sea, not in the Queen's ships – denied to him in any case as he had already been placed on the half-pay list – but to gain experience of merchant ships with a view to buying himself his own vessel which he would sail as owner-master.

Halfhyde had jumped at it. The sea was his life, Mildred his incubus. Uncle Henry had detested his own niece, and had little more love for his pompous brother or his sour-faced sister-in-law. A country squire in Hampshire, Uncle Henry was a lover of life who found himself at one with Halfhyde's restlessness in an intolerable situation. The money – it was to be a loan, repayable when Halfhyde felt able to – had not been sought; it had been freely and generously offered . . .

'And you have a ship in mind,' William Sturt said, breaking into Halfhyde's thoughts.

'Yes, indeed I have. I shall be seeing Captain Good this very afternoon. She's a trim ship, small but sound, and I count myself lucky. Having bought her, all I shall need is a cargo.'

2

'And there's the rub, as you'll find.' Sturt, a short, stout man, reached up and laid a hand on Halfhyde's shoulder. 'I wish you luck, Captain Halfhyde —'

'A little early for the captain, Mr. Sturt. I am not yet the owner, nor the master.'

'You're a master mariner.'

'A certificate of service following upon my years in the Queen's ships – not a certificate of competency.'

'It comes to the same thing.'

Halfhyde nodded. 'Officially, yes. It won't satisfy me, however. I feel it has yet to be earned.'

'I wouldn't worry about that,' Sturt said. 'Worry about your cargo – and maybe a passenger or two. Passengers are better payers in these times, Captain, though many a master dislikes them. Cargo doesn't eat, complain and give itself airs and graces. Passengers, one has to admit, do all three. But you have to live.'

* * *

Halfhyde thought: yes, you have to live. Live he would; he would not be beaten before he started. A cargo would be found. His months in Sydney, interrupted by a couple of voyages in a coaster trading across the Great Australian Bight to Fremantle on the Swan River, had not been idle ones. He had made a number of contacts in shipping and exporting circles and had mingled with the wharfies in the docks of Sydney, Melbourne and Fremantle, picking up all manner of useful scraps of knowledge, getting to know the Australians. That had been an uphill task; the pommies always had to prove themselves in Australian eyes. At the start all pommies tended to be regarded as hoity-toity remittance men, loafers, bad eggs or just plain bums. Australia was a man's country, however, and that suited Halfhyde, suffering from a surfeit of marriage and a mother-in-law like a vinegar bottle. He had made friends both high and low. Yes, a cargo would come.

After leaving the reception at Government House, Halfhyde walked down to the berths at Circular Quay. Like Liverpool, Sydney was a seaman's town. It held more than twenty-three

3

miles of quays and wharves able to load and discharge the
largest vessels afloat. The trade of the port stood at upwards of
twenty million pounds a year and there should be pickings for
an energetic owner-master out of such a sum. Coming down to
the quay Halfhyde stopped for a moment and looked at the ss
Taronga Park, shortly to be his. Small – as he had said to Sturt –
she was of no more than 1,400 net register tons, with raised
fo'c'sle, centre superstructure and poop, and the cargo holds in
between. A thin funnel rose abaft the bridge, black-painted.
The upperworks were painted a dull brown, the hull black with
green boot-topping. The engine, which was of the inverted
vertical direct-acting variety, drove a single screw that would
propel her through the water at a maximum speed of ten knots.
Her furnaces would need to be fed; coal was not cheap. The
price stood currently at around five shillings a ton. Had
Halfhyde gone for sail, the wind would have been free; but free
wind to drive a half-empty ship was not a good business
proposition. The shippers were turning more and more to
steam rather than sail for their exports, for the steamships
made their passages faster and time was money. The windjammers, as the last decade of the nineteenth century ran
towards its close, were beginning to lose even the wool trade for
London.

Halfhyde moved on, halted again alongside the *Taronga Park*
at the quay. As he looked up at her with an already
proprietorial air, an old man, white-haired, came out from a
doorway on the master's deck immediately below the bridge.

Halfhyde took off his hat. 'Good afternoon, Captain Good.'

'So you've come.'

'I'm sorry.'

'Never mind that. You'd better step aboard, Mister.'

Halfhyde did so. The gangway was spotless, as was the rest
of the ship and her fittings. She was recently in from a coasting
voyage; Captain Good, the vendor, had not remained wholly
harbour bound while the negotiations with Halfhyde had
proceeded. He couldn't afford to and wouldn't have wanted to.
Good was sixty-nine years of age and had been fifty-four years
at sea. He didn't want to go ashore but age and illness had

4

caught up with him; though the doctors didn't know what was the matter, he had developed a shake in his limbs and a feeling of constant lassitude, and he knew he couldn't go on commanding a ship for much longer. So he had accepted the inevitable and put his ship up for sale. To its owner-master, the *Taronga Park* was not just his ship and his livelihood: it was his home. Halfhyde understood the wrench. He had had many a talk with Captain Good the last few weeks, over glasses of Old Soldier rum. There was no wife, never had been; Captain Good had been married to the sea. His retirement would be spent in the home of his widowed sister in a small house in Balmain. He didn't look forward to it. His sister sounded like a muted Mildred. Where Mildred's one interest was horses, the Captain's sister was interested solely in church matters, and to pass the time when not actually in church she stuffed hassocks.

'Bloody penance it's going to be,' Captain Good had said when the question came up. 'But with luck it'll not last long. She'll have me in my grave in no time, that's for sure.'

'There's always the rum.'

'Aye! When she's not around to smell it. Her or the parson. Parson's got a nose on him like a customs rummager.'

Thinking of this and other conversations, Halfhyde followed Captain Good into his cabin, the cabin soon to be his own. He tried not to look too hard at things he would wish to change. It wouldn't matter afterwards: Good, he suspected, would never wish to set foot aboard again. Memories were best kept intact. The Captain told him to be seated, and brought out the rum bottle, pouring a sizeable amount with a hand that shook like an aspen but somehow managed to get the liquor into both glasses without spilling a drop. It was a slow process, however.

Halfhyde raised his glass. 'Good health, sir.'

'It's too late for that, Mister,' Good said bitterly. Halfhyde wished his tongue had been more tactful; there were other toasts. 'So you have the money.'

'Yes. It will be paid over as promptly as you wish. But you must take your time, sir.'

Good shook his head. 'No, I'll not do that. You're raring to come aboard as master, and as for me, the cleaner and sooner

5

the break the better. It'll take time for the formalities to be gone through since officialdom spends its days on its bottom, but I'll cause no delays, you may be sure.'

'Thank you, sir.'

'And my crew. You'll take them?'

'If they wish to join me. On your past recommendations, I'll sign them all.'

'I don't know about recommendations,' Good said. 'They're as fair as you'll ever get these days. The mates are all right .. . . the fo'c'sle crowd's a mixed bag like all fo'c'sle crowds. You can trust the bosun. You can nearly always trust bosuns.' His shaking hand brushed spilled birdseed from the cabin table's green baize cloth. From a hook in the deckhead where a lamp might have been expected to hang there hung instead a birdcage containing a canary, its beak probing a small china feeding bowl fixed to the bars. There was a little birdseed in Halfhyde's rum. A goldfish swam in circles in a glass bowl on the roll-top desk. Goldfish and canary would presumably leave the ship with Captain Good. Good went on, 'Don't know about engineers. I have to admit I don't like them.'

'I know you regretted leaving sail, sir,' Halfhyde said.

Good passed a hand over his forehead. He had told Halfhyde that he had lost his ship – not his fault, that had been proved – broken up on the Barrier Reef. He had got the insurance money and borrowed some more . . . it had seemed only sensible to go for steam with sail cargoes dropping away. Now he said, 'I didn't like it, I can tell you, but a man must eat. That was four years ago. I've never got really used to not being in a windjammer. Some ways, that makes the break the easier now.'

* * *

Halfhyde walked along Macquarie Street, turned off half-way up, entered a building and climbed a flight of stairs. He went into a waiting room and banged on the frosted glass of a hatch. A head appeared: Halfhyde had an appointment with a Mr Matthews. He was kept waiting for almost half an hour. When he was shown to a private office he said, 'I've bought, or am about to buy, the *Taronga Park*. Now I want a cargo.'

6

Matthews smiled. 'Not as easy as that, Captain.'

'I understood you could accommodate me?'

'Sure – at the time. Just now, there's nothing. The mail boat took the lot. I'm sorry, but there it is. Keep in touch – call round again and there may be something, but no promises. A lot of masters are in the same boat, you know.'

That was that. Halfhyde took his leave. He visited other shipping agents and exporters' offices and the story was the same. The mail boat had beaten him to it and a good deal of forward shipping had been bespoken for the next mail boat due in from the London River. There was nothing left for a small steamer. Contact after contact failed him; all the earlier, airy promises were seen as dross. Once the purchase money had been paid over, Halfhyde would have but a narrow margin, enough to coal and store his ship for London and little else. The portage bill, record of crew wages and other payments, loomed. Men didn't go to sea for nothing. By the week's end gloom had settled like a pall. Halfhyde had never expected such a series of brick walls; even the contacts passed on by Captain Good had come to nothing. They might all have at least a part cargo soon, but currently there was nothing doing.

Other ships, both sail and steam, were getting cargoes. Halfhyde watched them loading at the wharves, bale after bale of wool going aboard, plus general cargoes. More and more desperately he tramped the streets. Perhaps he would have better luck in another port – Melbourne, Adelaide, Fremantle, even Brisbane. Since his arrival in Australia he'd been told by more than one person that as a pommie he might face difficulty. When it came to the small ships sailed by their owners, the Australians gave priority to their own countrymen.

He hadn't believed it then. He'd been too confident, too euphoric.

Perhaps he should have accepted the dead weight of Mildred; perhaps he should have thrown Uncle Henry's generosity back in his teeth, returned to England, humbly besought the Admiralty to grant him back his commission and waited for them to offer him a lieutenant's appointment aboard a Queen's ship, patiently bearing his conjugal cross until that time came. But his innermost being told him that Mildred was an impossible alternative and that to go back would be to deliver himself lock, stock and barrel into Willard hands, the returned prodigal with his tail between his legs. No: he would not go back. His bed made, he would lie on it. And he could not, would not go back on his purchase.

As soon as the formalities and the documentation were complete Halfhyde paid over the purchase money in the shipbroker's office and when he and Captain Good walked back together to the *Taronga Park*, Halfhyde went aboard as master. For good or ill, it was done. Captain Halfhyde: it was a satisfactory sound in his ears, even if he was on the verge of bankruptcy.

After a glass of rum he walked to the gangway with the white-haired old man, who was shaking more than ever and suddenly very frail, as though parting with his ship was bringing him close to his end. Even the canary looked depressed, forbearing to peck its seed as it swayed in its cage. In Good's other hand was the goldfish in its bowl. To Halfhyde it looked dead, floating upside down, with a white look about it. He remarked on this.

'Too bloody right,' Captain Good said sadly. 'It's those customs people, the buggers. They go into everything . . . I had some gin to keep away from them. Easier to hide than rum. I'd filled all me jugs and glasses, still had some over as a matter of fact . . . then I filled the bloody goldfish bowl from a jug by mistake.'

Halfhyde blew out his cheeks in sympathy. 'And the fish —?'

'Too right,' Captain Good said. 'He'll have a decent burial in Balmain, though.' Shoulders bowed, the old man turned away, close to tears; then turned back, put down the canary and sketched a salute towards the house flag designed by Halfhyde and made for him by a ship's chandler down by Circular Quay. A blue flag with a large white H in its centre, it floated on a breeze from the mainmast head. The Halfhyde Line . . . that was to be the name. Captain Good took Halfhyde's hand and said, 'May you succeed to own a dozen fine ships, Captain. I wish you well.'

8

Halfhyde smiled. 'I would you could wish me a cargo, sir.'

'Yes. I understand very well. Myself, I had no forward cargo for another voyage. If I had done so, it would have been yours, of course.' Captain Good paused, hand shaking on the rail. 'I wonder . . . do you know a man called Porteous Higgins?'

'No.'

'Go and see him. Shop in Porch Street, in the Cross. He's sometimes of help, so I'm told. I've not had dealings with him myself. I understand he needs watching. But when you're in desperate straits it's a case of any Porteous in a storm!'

On the heels of his witticism Captain Good went down the gangway without a backward look and got into a shabby victoria, to be driven to his sister's home and a slow descent into sanctity, senility and hassocks. When he had gone, Halfhyde strode about his ship, noting things that he would wish to have done when he had the money. He strode unaccompanied; there was only a watchman aboard. Next morning he would attend at the shipping office to sign his crew on articles. For the rest of this day he had little to do but ponder on Porteous Higgins and go ashore in another despairing attempt to find a cargo. There was still nothing for the *Taronga Park*.

Porteous Higgins was the last resort and the time had come. Now that Halfhyde was the owner of the *Taronga Park* he would have to meet the harbour dues: each day in port cost money.

TWO

The Cross, as the Kings Cross district of Sydney was more familiarly known, was a down-at-heel area inhabited largely by prostitutes; and bars proliferated. It had a kind of charm; the buildings were small and old, set close together in narrow streets and alleys, and there was a friendliness, a matiness that was not so apparent in the busier commercial purlieus of Castlereagh Street, Macquarie Street and the rest. At the same time, in some parts of the Cross, there was an aura of something approaching evil. It was an area of crime; and Halfhyde was under no illusions as to the probable shady dealings that would be connected with Porteous Higgins. But he was between the devil and the deep blue sea and Higgins would at least be worth talking to. The greasing of a few palms, Higgins' naturally included, could perhaps bring about a miracle and produce a cargo. Halfhyde knew he was a novice, a child in the shipping business, and never mind his years at sea in the Queen's ships – there was a world of difference between the profession of a seaman and the financial wheelings and dealings of a ship-owner. Over the past weeks bribery had in fact been hinted at discreetly by men in shipping offices and agencies, but Halfhyde, accustomed to the ways of the Queen's service, had steadfastly set his face against all such hints.

Until now: needs must, he thought as he strode through the seedy thoroughfares towards Porch Street, pursued by urchins, called at by women seated at open windows, negligently dressed so as to display at least a promise of their wares.

He found Porch Street; it was seedier than the others, narrow and smelly. There were Greek shops, Italian shops and Chinese shops – selling groceries and leather work, books and paintings – cheek by jowl with one another, staring into the eyes of those opposite. Porteous Higgins' establishment carried his name painted above a display of cheap jewellery, trinkets mostly, brooches and beads and cameos hung from thin chains of gold or gilt.

Halfhyde looked at the display and saw, beyond in the shop's interior, a woman studying him from behind a counter.

He went inside, opening a door that caused a bell to tinkle above his head. The shop was stuffy with the heat of the day and the sweat of the woman custodian.

Halfhyde cleared his throat and fanned his face with his hat. 'It's close,' he said.

'If you don't like it you can get out.' She smiled at him nevertheless. 'You want to buy something?'

Halfhyde moved closer. The woman was not unattractive; she had a good figure and the eyes were large and dark, the skin golden. A vision of Mildred floated before him: the contrast was cruel. Feelings stirred in his body, but he subdued them. This was business, vital to his survival in a difficult world. He said, 'I may decide to buy something. First, I'd appreciate a word with Mr Higgins if he's available.'

'He could be, I reckon,' the woman said. 'What's your business?'

'Shipping.'

'Name?'

'Captain Halfhyde, of the *Taronga Park*.'

'*Taronga Park*, eh? What's happened to old Jakey Good, then?'

Halfhyde said, 'He's retired. I've bought the ship.'

'Gone to live with that sister of his, has he?'

'Yes.'

The woman gave a peal of laughter. 'Poor old sod.'

Halfhyde, recalling that Captain Good had denied having had any dealings himself with Porteous Higgins, remarked, 'You seem to know a lot about ships and shipmasters. How is that?'

The woman gave him a wink. 'You want to talk to Mr Higgins, don't you? You're not the only shipmaster that's done that, and there's always gossip about other captains and their ships, see? Jakey Good's been around a long while.'

'But not here.'

'Not to see Mr Higgins,' the woman said. She gave another ringing peal of laughter and Halfhyde read the message in the dark, seductive eyes. Well, well; he wouldn't have suspected it; Captain Good had appeared too desiccated for such things. Now there was another reason for Good's reluctance to live with his sister: he would be watched like a hawk in case he brought disrepute upon the church. The woman spoke again. 'Hang on a minute,' she said, 'and don't pinch the stock while I'm gone. I'll ask if Mr Higgins can see you.'

She went through a door in rear of the counter, closing it behind her. Even had he wished to pinch the displayed trinkets he would have had no chance. Throughout the conversation he had been aware of watching eyes behind a thin slit high up in a wall. The woman was not gone long. Coming back she said Mr Higgins could spare him a moment. 'Through there,' she said, indicating the door she had herself used. 'Straight down the passage, door at the end on the right.'

'Thank you.'

She waved a hand. 'That's quite all right, Captain.' The eyes said she would be there when he had finished with Higgins and wouldn't be found stand-offish. He went through, found the door at the end, and knocked. A voice bade him enter. Porteous Higgins was seated at a kneehole desk. He got to his feet as Halfhyde came in. They shook hands. Higgins was a big man, fleshy and powerful; the face was heavy, with a pendulous lower lip and rolls of chins beneath, overflowing his hard collar. He was coatless, and gold bands held back the cuffs of his shirt from his wrists. There was a smell of garlic in the air.

'How do,' he said. 'Name of Halfhyde, I'm told.'

'That's right, Mr Higgins.'

'What's your business?'

Halfhyde came straight to the point. 'I'm in need of a cargo.'

'Yes,' Higgins said as though he'd known all along. 'Sit

12

down, Captain.'

They both sat. Halfhyde asked, 'What are the chances you'll be able to help?'

Higgins was looking him up and down, the eyes narrowed, almost invisible in the rolls of flesh screwed up around the sockets. 'Why do you think I might?'

Halfhyde said, 'Your name was mentioned to me by my predecessor.'

'Jakey Good. I see. *Taronga Park*. I know the ship. She's seaworthy—'

'Of course,' Halfhyde interrupted with asperity. 'Had she not been, I wouldn't have bought her. I happen to know my way about a ship.

Higgins smiled. 'Yes, indeed. Your service in the Royal Navy—'

'You know about that?' Halfhyde was astonished.

'Yes. One moment.' Higgins opened a drawer in his desk and brought out a sheet of paper covered with neat writing, a clerk's hand. 'Lieutenant St Vincent Halfhyde, lately upon the half-pay list of the Royal Navy, now retired. Held command of Her Majesty's ships *Vendetta* and *Talisman*. Also served aboard the battleships *Prince Consort* and *Meridian*, and the monitor *Lord Cochrane*, among other ships. More recently signed aboard the sailing ship *Aysgarth Falls* as able-bodied seaman, being advanced for divers reasons to the rank of First Mate before the voyage from Liverpool ended here in Sydney. Captain McRafferty released you from the ship's articles so that you could look for a vessel to purchase in Australia.' Higgins laid the sheet of paper down on the desk. 'Am I right, Captain Halfhyde?'

'Yes,' Halfhyde said curtly. 'May I ask how and why you obtained this information about me?'

Higgins shrugged. He lit a cigar and blew smoke across the room towards Halfhyde. Its aroma began to overlay the garlic. 'I make it my business to acquire knowledge of all shipmasters and first mates using the port, Captain. More particularly, of those aspiring to become owner-masters, as in your case. It is not hard to get access to such information as I want. As regards yourself for instance, there is such a thing as the Navy List, as I needn't remind you – and there is always gossip in seafaring circles, in the clubs and bars. Such gossip gives one the first hints, and then to follow up is easy.'

'I asked why,' Halfhyde said with an edge to his voice.

Higgins smiled and spread large, hammy hands. 'Because in some cases I can be of use. In such cases there is mutual profit – and I am a businessman. I see nothing wrong in that.'

'Perhaps not. But it's almost as though you were expecting me to come to see you, Mr Higgins.'

'Many people come to see me.'

'No doubt. I'd be obliged if you'd tell me whether or not you're in a position to help me in regard to cargo for London or *en route* ports.'

Porteous Higgins continued to stare at him for some moments, then said, 'It's very possible, Captain. Very possible. I happen to know of a consignment for the United Kingdom – not in this case for the London River, but for the port of Queenstown in Ireland.'

'And the nature of the consignment?'

'Cased machine parts,' Porteous Higgins said.

'One more question: who is the shipper?'

'Myself, Captain.' Higgins was bland. 'When do you expect to sail?'

Halfhyde said, 'Having got myself a cargo, if the terms are right that is, I shall sail just as soon as that cargo's brought aboard. Arrangements have been made to sign my crew tomorrow morning, and after that I shall be ready to take cargo.'

Higgins nodded. 'Excellent, Captain. Now we shall discuss terms.' He raised his eyebrows. 'You'll take some whisky?'

'Thank you.'

* * *

Porteous Higgins' whisky was good and the terms seemed fair. The bargain was struck, the cargo manifest produced. Halfhyde signed documents where indicated by Higgins. As an apparent afterthought Higgins mentioned, casually enough, that the cargo would not be loaded at the wharf in Port Jackson but would be transferred at sea, from two coasters that would rendezvous with the *Taronga Park* outside the Great Barrier Reef, to seaward of the Northumberland Islands at a time to be announced later.

That was when Halfhyde smelt the rat.

He asked, 'Have you approached any other agents or masters in regard to your cargo?'

'I have not.'

'Then why choose my ship?'

Higgins smiled. 'The answer to that, Captain, is that it's your sheer luck. It so happens that I bought up some stock this very morning, having a ready buyer in—'

'Cased machine parts, you said?'

'Yes.'

'For Ireland. And cased machine parts is a fairly all-embracing description, I fancy. Ireland is a troubled land, Mr Higgins.' Halfhyde was thinking of past atrocities, of the Irish self-styled patriots who had raided Chester Castle back in sixty-seven, and who in the same year had attacked the police in Manchester, to say nothing of shootings and ambushes in Ireland itself, the constant internecine warfare between the men of the Fenian Society and the British soldiers at the Curragh and other military establishments, the cowardly murders of the men of the Royal Irish Constabulary. It was common knowledge that the Fenian Men, as they were called, had been frequently supplied with arms from outside the United Kingdom. 'I shall want a more detailed description of the cargo before I agree—'

'You have had the description, Captain.' Higgins' eyes had narrowed and his face had taken on an ugly look. He rose to his feet. 'I have nothing to add.'

'Then I am sorry, but I shall not take it—'

'May I remind you that you've already signed documents agreeing to accept my cargo manifest?'

'For the first time in my life,' Halfhyde said, himself rising to face Higgins, 'I shall go back upon my signature. I shall have none of your cargo without—'

15

'Don't make an enemy of me, Halfhyde. You would very much regret that. I have friends in high places – remember that. Remember that you're committed, too. And there's another thing. Your voyage north to the Barrier Reef will not be your first experience of that region, will it? We've already spoken of Captain McRafferty of the *Aysgarth Falls*. You'll not have forgotten his passenger, the deserter and murderer Sergeant Cantlow?'

Halfhyde's fists clenched and he took a step forward. The memories were all too recent. McRafferty was a good man, taken advantage of by an evil First Mate – Bullock, now dead. Bullock had been killed off the Barrier Reef by Cantlow, the passenger he himself had brought aboard in expectation of a share in the proceeds of a diamond smuggling operation out of South Africa. Halfhyde said, 'You can make nothing of that, Higgins. It's past history. McRafferty and I are both in the clear.'

'You made an attempt to assist a murderer to evade justice.'

'I said we're in—'

'I'm aware of what you said, Halfhyde. It cuts no ice – or won't if you cross me. I can have the enquiry re-opened, and you charged, and McRafferty too when his ship comes into Sydney again. Ponder on it, Halfhyde. If you go to the police, you're finished. Think well, and then you'll see the advantages of co-operation. I'm not taking you for a fool. There's little risk in it for you.'

'You've mistaken your man,' Halfhyde said coldly. He turned away from Porteous Higgins. There was nothing to be gained by a rough-house. He walked out in a fury, leaving the door open behind him. He was aware of Porteous Higgins' bulky figure coming out into the passage. He half expected a physical attack but none came; no doubt Higgins kept himself aloof from such things. He would have hired thugs to do that sort of work. Halfhyde swept past the woman in the shop without a word. She stared after him, looking disappointed. Halfhyde tended to catch the female eye: tall, spare, no stomach, hard muscles, the lean and cadaverous look. As Halfhyde banged out into the street Porteous Higgins spoke to

the woman.

'He'll come to heel soon,' he said.

'You going to put the boys on him?' She sounded regretful.

'Not unless he asks for it,' Porteous Higgins said.

* * *

Halfhyde was convinced his unspoken diagnosis had been correct: arms for would-be rebels in Ireland. The man's manner, the fact that he had uttered threats, all confirmed Halfhyde's belief. But Higgins had undoubtedly mistaken his man and at first Halfhyde was amazed at what appeared to be an elementary and stupid error of judgement on the part of Higgins. One who had held the Queen's commission would scarcely be likely to throw in his lot with gun-runners to a set of bog-dwellers, dissidents, murderers and doers of treason. But, as he walked away from the Cross towards the Domain, Halfhyde's reflections showed him a different and more understandable angle. Men like Porteous Higgins would fail to understand the loyalty that accompanied an officer into retirement. Once an officer of the Queen you remained such until death. Even the unemployed list was part of the Navy. An officer never relinquished his commission unless he had been drummed out by sentence of a court martial, dropped by Her Majesty in disgrace. Such had not happened to Halfhyde, but Porteous Higgins might well think him a harbourer of disloyal thoughts. It was very possible that Higgins was in possession of other facts of Halfhyde's Naval career: the constant asperity with senior officers whom he had considered fools, the disobedience to orders that he had frequently shown, his habit of speaking his mind without fear of admirals, his periods on the half-pay list because he had upset high authority – none of these were popularly considered to be the mark of the dedicated career officer. His early retirement, his intense dislike of his father-in-law Vice-Admiral Willard, his virtual desertion of that high officer's daughter, all added up, if Higgins was aware of it, to something that might well have given the fellow a distorted view of Halfhyde's integrity when added to his desperate and impoverished search for a cargo – which for a certainty Higgins would also have heard through his many ears.

Well, so Higgins had made a mistake. He would have to pay for it. A word in the right quarter would see that he did. The police?

Perhaps, perhaps not. Bribery could be very widespread indeed. Even the police were not immune.

Halfhyde pulled out his watch, studied it and went into a handy hotel. He called for a glass of whisky, using the bar rather than the lounge. Halfhyde was no lover of hotel lounges or of ladies' drawing-rooms either: they were stultified by good manners and etiquette. He had passed the lounge on the way to the bar: he had glimpsed two or three young men in rigidly correct attire paying polite court to young women of varying degrees of attraction while the young women's grim-jawed mothers acted as chaperons, eagle-eyed for hanky-panky in word or act. The glimmer in an eye, the movement of a hand towards another – gloved – hand would no doubt constitute hanky-panky enough in those terrible dowagers' minds.

The bar was more cosmopolitan and down to earth. Halfhyde recognized the stamp of seafarers, masters and mates from the ships lying in Port Jackson, luckier perhaps than he with the availability of cargoes. They seemed mostly to know one another; Halfhyde, finding no familiar face, was odd man out and he drank alone in a corner. Once he heard the name of Porteous Higgins mentioned, though he didn't catch the reference – and the speaker, having spoken, stared round himself as if fearing to be overheard.

The law could prove a trap. Porteous Higgins would be able to look after himself and the facts were plain: Halfhyde had entered into a contract and was therefore a *prima facie* confederate – a confederate who perhaps had fallen out with his shipper and was acting from malice. In the meantime the cargo would be well out of the way of prying eyes; Halfhyde didn't know even the names of the coasters that were to steal out from behind the Barrier Reef.

Mr William Sturt of the Australian Joint Stock Bank might well be the man to go to. His contacts, too, were wide; and he knew his Sydney. Halfhyde finished his whisky and left the hotel. Outside, some way down the road and reading a newspaper, was a man Halfhyde had seen before he had entered. Not yet spotted, he turned the other way and went down a side street into the next main street. He hailed a horse-drawn cab and gave the address of Sturt's home: by now the day's work would have ended. He found Sturt sitting on a wide verandah with a decanter of sherry on a table beside him. Sturt, a bachelor, was alone; when the abo servant who had admitted him had gone, Halfhyde came straight out with his story.

Sturt was obviously uneasy. 'Sounds like dirty work,' he said. 'But you've no proof the cases contain anything other than is stated in the manifest, have you?'

'None. But the juxtaposition of the facts speaks for itself. An Irish port and a clandestine loading. The use of my ship, the belief being that I'm an inexperienced shipmaster – which I admit I am. The way Higgins, who presumably is Irish, made a point of bringing up the *Aysgarth Falls* business—'

'An attempt at getting a hold over you. Yes, I agree.'

'So what's to be done about it?'

Sturt stroked his chin; Halfhyde noticed a shake in his fingers. There was no answer to his question. He continued: 'The police, the port authorities?'

'You'd get nowhere, Halfhyde. Porteous Higgins spreads a very wide net – but don't quote me on that. I'd like to help myself, but . . .'

'Yes?'

'It would be too bloody indiscreet,' Sturt said with an air of finality. 'At times, Sydney can be a lawless place.'

* * *

Halfhyde had instructed the cab to wait; he went back in it to Circular Quay, keeping his eyes open throughout the drive. Sturt had been no help at all; his inferences had been obvious: the knife in the back was a reality in Sydney Town, and Porteous Higgins had a lot of people in his pocket. Sturt among them? Halfhyde wondered about that. Sturt's house was big, standing in extensive grounds, and was well staffed. He

maintained a carriage and pair and all that went with all of that
. . . very obvious affluence, but then that could be expected of a
director of the Joint Stock Bank, of course. Probably innocent of
corruption, but still fearful for his life if he got up against
Porteous Higgins from the sleazy cheap-jack jeweller's shop in
the Cross.

And he'd refused to become involved, hadn't liked being
approached in the first place. He wanted his name kept right
out of it henceforward. He had handled Halfhyde's finance and
that was as far as he was going to be involved. Without being
too precise in words, he had conveyed all that pretty clearly.
His advice had been simple: go along with Porteous Higgins
and deal with the matter at the other end. If necessary, steam
the *Taronga Park* nowhere near Ireland but into the English
Channel, make the London River with his cargo, and then
render his report.

That could be sound sense but it held dangers. Firstly, if
anything should go wrong with the clandestine loading operation, Halfhyde would be in a very exposed position vis-à-vis
the Australian authorities. Secondly, Halfhyde was in no doubt
that Porteous Higgins would have thought for himself of a
possible deviation from his destination and would have taken
steps to cover it. There was another aspect: Sturt had
confirmed that there was no ban on arms exports or re-exports
from Australia. Respectable arms dealers could ship their
consignments where they could make a sale. Jiggery-pokery
was not necessary. It was obvious that Porteous Higgins, and
through him Halfhyde, was dealing in stolen goods.

At the bottom of George Street Halfhyde paid off the cab and
walked on to the quay. He looked ahead at the *Taronga Park*.
Despite his worries, he felt the surge of pride: his own ship, his
own house flag . . . she needed a coat of paint but that could
wait. There was much ocean to cross and she would arrive in
the United Kingdom looking seaworn whatever was done to
her down here in the southland, the land of the Southern Cross
and the deep-hanging stars. What had to be done would be best
done in the London docks, or more probably, for his pocket's
sake, a smaller port such as Falmouth. The world over, capital

cities tended to bring high prices.

He climbed the gangway: no watchman in sight. Well, as from tomorrow when his full crew would be signed, all slackness would cease. The watchman, a locally engaged Sydneysider, would not be sailing with the ship in any case. Halfhyde, his mind reverting to Porteous Higgins and the problems he had brought, forbore to shout for the watchman and give him a piece of his mind. He went straight to his cabin. Some sixth sense told him, before he had brought out his keys to unlock the door, that he was no longer alone. Then he heard the footsteps on the ladder leading down from the bridge, and he turned, and there was the woman.

They stared at each other. Halfhyde's eyebrows went up. The woman – who now looked to be in her late twenties – said, 'I thought you'd maybe want some company, Captain, after all.'

'I've already gathered you're familiar with the ship.'

'Jakey Good?' She gave a sudden surge of laughter. 'You're right – up to a point. Jakey Good, it was mostly just the company he wanted. Mostly. Christ, he used to talk, hour after hour, all about the places he'd seen.' She paused, her dark eyes assessing him. 'How about you, Captain?'

'I'm not much of a talker,' Halfhyde said. The woman attracted him; her supple body, the look in the eyes, the well-formed breasts . . . and he was no plaster saint. He felt his increased pulse, the undeniable attraction. He pushed from his mind the possibility that to accept her advances might be to compromise himself even more in some obscure way. Porteous Higgins could be presumed to own this woman, but for this night Porteous Higgins was going to be forgotten. His mind ran over prosaic practicalities: the woman would want to eat, and currently he had no facilities. He hadn't yet even shifted his gear aboard; he was still living in lodgings until the ship had her crew aboard. You didn't pay men to hang around a ship in port, not till she was ready to load. He said, 'A meal together ashore. I shall treat you. Then we shall come back aboard.'

* * *

That night, Halfhyde was prodigal with his money: the meal for two, with whisky and the tip, cost him a sovereign in a hotel in Castlereagh Street. They went back in style, in a cab, though the distance was not great. A guard lantern was lit at the gangway, and this time the watchman was in evidence, sitting gnarled and surly on a folding canvas stool on the fore well-deck.

'On your feet, man,' Halfhyde said sharply.

The ancient fellow stared but made no move. 'What did yer sye?'

'I think you heard. When a lady and your Captain come aboard, you get to your feet – sharp! Unless you wish to be thrown into the harbour for a cruising shark to crunch your old bones.'

The man got up. 'That's better,' Halfhyde said, and stalked on behind the woman towards the ladder to his cabin. He half regretted his sharpness to an old man, but proper discipline must be maintained from the start. Start as you mean to go on, the Queen's service had taught him, and the lesson had been well learned. Even a shoreside watchman could pass things on to a ship's crew and an easy captain would be taken immediate advantage of.

Forgoing light, Halfhyde took the woman in his arms in his cabin's darkness. Lights from the shore flickered yellowish through his port, throwing shadows on the white-painted bulkhead above the bunk. The woman's breath came fast as he eased the clothing from her and she felt his body against her. He lifted her on to the bunk and laid her gently down, thinking suddenly and irreverently of Captain Good and his shaking limbs. But Captain Good had mostly talked; there was little talking that night. In the end came sleep, then an awakening in a bath of sweat as the dawn's light stole through the port. Sydney could be a hot place.

The woman – he had discovered her name was Victoria Penn – left early. She had to be at the shop in Porch Street. Never once had she mentioned Porteous Higgins and neither had Halfhyde. He had deliberately not probed, knowing that he wouldn't get the truth in any case. Also, word of any probing could have been assumed to reach the ear of Porteous Higgins.

Halfhyde didn't want that; realizing that he faced a brick wall in Sydney he had made up his mind to the best alternative – that proposed by Mr William Sturt. Back in Britain, he would be on firm ground. And he would back himself to deal firmly with the cargo too.

At 11 am that day he was waiting at the shipping office for his crew to arrive and for the shipping master to open the fresh articles of agreement for the *Taronga Park* bound for the United Kingdom. Most of the crew he had met already, whilst paying his visits to Captain Good. They were mostly Australian, since the ship's home port was Sydney, but the First Mate, Herbert Perry, was as English as Halfhyde himself. Perry was the first to arrive after Halfhyde.

'Good morning, Mr Perry.'

'Good morning, sir. I hope all hands are sober enough to sign.'

'Yes. If they're not, you know how to deal with them when you get them aboard.'

Perry grinned. 'Yes, sir. Wash-deck hoses. Cleans and sobers at one and the same time.'

Mr Baird, Chief Engineer, was the next to turn up and Halfhyde greeted him with reserve. Engineers were awkward men to deal with and Halfhyde had already reckoned Angus Baird from Clydeside, another of the non-Australians, to be as awkward as any if not more so. But his words with his Chief Engineer were friendly enough; and they were interrupted by an unexpected arrival.

Porteous Higgins came through the door. He was not alone; he was accompanied by a squat man – a hairy man with over-long and very powerful arms and a deep chest like a barrel. When introduced, the name fitted the man well: Ed Gaboon. Porteous Higgins had called Halfhyde aside to make the introduction, and said, 'Gaboon is to be your steward, Captain.'

'He is not,' Halfhyde said. 'My steward is to be Captain Good's steward, about to be signed on.'

'On the contrary. I advise you not to argue and make trouble, Captain. I insist that Gaboon be signed on articles as your steward.'

'And if – when – I refuse?'

'Then there will be trouble, Captain, that I promise you.'

Halfhyde, furious at the attempted interference with his rights as master of the *Taronga Park*, stared with distaste at the squat, ape-like man. Higgins' ploy was all too obvious: Gaboon, Halfhyde's personal servant, was intended to be his warder, acting in Higgins' interest. There was no-one else aboard a ship who stood in the close relationship of a master's steward to the master. Halfhyde would be watched throughout the voyage. This was Porteous Higgins' way of ensuring that there was no change in his cargo's destination. The arms of Gaboon were killer's arms and he would probably be handy with a knife. With Gaboon behind him on the bridge as the *Taronga Park* raised the Fastnet he would be given no chance unless he wished to die. Very likely others of his crew would be in Higgins' pay: he would be able to trust no-one to relieve him of Gaboon, once aboard.

Halfhyde stared Higgins in the face, his back straight, his long chin out-thrust. 'I shall not take him. I refuse to sign this man. That is my last word.'

He turned about and stalked back to the shipping master's table. When next he looked towards the door Porteous Higgins and his dangerous-looking ally had gone. But Halfhyde had no confidence that he had seen the last of Ed Gaboon.

THREE

With the crew aboard, there was much to do: Captain Good's last run had been to Newcastle, NSW, where he had taken a cargo of Hunter River coal. The holds had to be cleaned down and Mr Perry, together with the bosun, saw to it right away. Sides, bulkheads and deckheads were swept down and the sweepings sent up on deck for disposal. Then the hoses were rigged and everything was washed down. The limber boards were lifted, the bilges cleaned out below and given a cement wash. The rose boxes were examined, the limber boards replaced, the holds dunnaged to take the fresh cargo, as were the tween-decks, the tween-deck dunnaging being laid athwartships to help the drainage of any water that might enter; and shifting boards were rigged.

It all took time; Perry was a conscientious First Mate. But at last sailing time came, with no interference from Porteous Higgins. But for Halfhyde, the thought of Higgins spoiled the moment.

* * *

Five days after passing Sydney Heads outwards into the blue brilliance of the Pacific Ocean, the *Taronga Park* was lying off to seaward of the Barrier Reef in the latitude of the Northumberland Islands. The day was fine, the sea disturbed only by a low swell, but enough to make the operation of transferring cargo a difficult one. Halfhyde lay with his engine stopped, awaiting the arrival of the coasters. The night before he had sailed, Victoria Penn had come aboard again, this time with

25

word from Porteous Higgins as to the exact time of the rendezvous. This time she had not stayed; her manner had been different – there was a wariness and a nervousness, an apparent anxiety to be away rather than to linger.

Halfhyde had suspected tantrums from Higgins after his rejection of the man Gaboon. He'd asked the question and got the confirmation. 'You were bloody stupid,' the woman said. 'Look, I don't want you to get hurt. There could be trouble.'

'Not after I'm clear of Port Jackson.'

'I wouldn't bet on it,' she said. She wouldn't say any more; that was when she left the ship. Now, up north off the Barrier Reef, Halfhyde had had plenty of time to ponder the little she'd said. A pound to a penny Gaboon would appear with the coasters, possibly with Higgins' authority to act as a sort of supercargo to watch the shipper's interests. Well, that could be dealt with too: Halfhyde would simply refuse permission for the man to board. Indeed, such would be so obvious to Higgins that perhaps he was unlikely to try it, but even so, Halfhyde still believed that Gaboon would manifest himself somewhere along the line, though only God could say how.

Halfhyde paced his bridge and stopped alongside the First Mate. 'They're late, Mr Perry.'

Perry was looking through a telescope. 'I believe they're coming out now, sir.' Halfhyde took up his own telescope. There was a smudge, very distant, well inside the coral.

'You may be right, Mr Perry.' Halfhyde waited, concealing his impatience, for a while longer. When it was plain that two small steamships were indeed coming out and were towing dumb lighters astern, he blew down the engine-room voice-pipe.

A Scots voice answered. 'Aye?'

'Captain here, Chief. We have the coasters coming off now.'

'How long before they reach us?'

Halfhyde said, 'Give it an hour. Steam on the windlass by then, please.'

There was no reply beyond an irritated grunt; the sound of Baird slamming back his voice-pipe cover rattled in Halfhyde's eardrums. He stepped back frowning. Baird had already

26

proved the prickliest of men, saw in every utterance from the bridge a reflection on his professional capabilities. Never mind: there were more important things to worry about than the asperity of an engineer from Clydeside. Halfhyde turned to the First Mate. 'Send down for Foster,' he said, naming the Second Mate. 'He's to relieve you while you make ready on deck.'

'Aye, aye, sir.' Perry, seeing the Second Mate walking for'ard from the poop, called to him. Foster came up nimbly and Perry went down the ladder and found the bosun, a middle-aged man named Matt Causton. They collected some hands and began the work of setting up the derricks to heave in the supposed cased machine parts from the lighters once the latter had been loaded and then dropped astern from the coasters.

'It's going to be a long job, sir,' Foster said.

'Yes, it is. Have you embarked a cargo at sea before?'

'No, sir.'

Halfhyde smiled. 'To be frank, no more have I. I shall learn by watching from the bridge, but you shall go below when the lighters are alongside to assist Mr Perry and gain experience. I shall take over the bridge watch.'

'Thank you, sir,' Foster said.

'You appear keen to learn and that's something I like to see. But I doubt if I shall ever take a cargo at sea again.'

'No, sir.' Foster said no more, but Halfhyde knew that every man aboard was curious about the sea-loading. He had had a talk with Perry about it, trying to reassure a plainly honest First Mate that there was no jiggery-pokery. That hadn't been easy, but Halfhyde, who had anticipated the natural queries, had had time to think something up. The shipper, he'd said, though having an office in Sydney – which Perry would have gleaned from the manifests – was despatching his cargo from Rockhampton and he, Halfhyde, having no knowledge of the Barrier Reef and being so far unused to the handling of a merchant ship, had preferred not to risk taking the *Taronga Park* in through the coral of the Barrier Reef. Just playing safe, he said. Perry had looked a little hurt, since he knew the reef well and could have handled the ship; Halfhyde was sorry about that but it couldn't be helped. He made a good deal of the fact that the ship was his own and he was taking no chances on a first voyage, however efficient and trustworthy his officers might be. Perry, in accepting that, would no doubt have passed it on, together with a comment or two on the Old Man's pernicketiness.

Slowly, with the dumb lighters in tow, the coasters began to close the *Taronga Park*. They came out through one of the safe channels to stand clear of the coral and when they were well into open water the lighters were hauled forward to lie alongside their towing vessels. The hatch covers were removed and then across the water Halfhyde could hear the rattle of steam winches. Derricks swung into position over the holds, the whips went down, and soon the first cases were coming up in the cargo nets, to be swung out over the lighters and grappled by hands sent down to stow them for the short run across to the *Taronga Park*. When the first coaster's master shouted across that he was ready, Halfhyde manoeuvred his ship into position astern of the dumb lighter, the coaster cast off the securing lines, and as it moved ahead Halfhyde followed in its wake, putting his ship alongside the lighter and sending down his lines to be made fast to the bitts.

He leaned from the bridge rail. 'All right, Mr Perry,' he called. 'Soon as you like now.'

Perry waved an acknowledgement and then lost no time. Halfhyde watched approvingly as the First Mate took firm charge: he looked like being good at his job. The sealed cases were brought inboard in the slings to be stowed directly into the fore hold. Another lighter load went into the after hold, then two more trips for each of the lighters and the holds were filled and the ship trimmed nicely in the water and well down to her marks.

Then something happened: something not totally unexpected by Halfhyde but highly unwelcome. One of the coasters moved towards the *Taronga Park*, laying so close alongside that Halfhyde shouted across to her master to have a care for his davits. There was no response beyond a shrug and a grin; and then Halfhyde saw the hairy thug, Gaboon, emerge on to the coaster's deck, run to her fo'c'sle as the bows nudged the

Taronga Park's fore well-deck, now low in the water, and jump across with a flying leap, landing on all fours, ape-like as ever. Gaboon turned to give a hand to another person: the woman from the Cross – and behind her Porteous Higgins.

* * *

Halfhyde was in a furious mood as he took the *Taronga Park* away from the Barrier Reef, headed on a course for Valparaiso in Chile. Porteous Higgins, when Halfhyde had threatened to throw him into the sea if he refused to go back aboard the coaster, had been smug. He had merely waved a hand towards the coaster's bridge. Looking, Halfhyde saw police uniforms. Higgins, smiling, had told him the sergeant in charge had a warrant for his arrest on charges brought in connection with the attempted clandestine landing in Australia of the murderer Cantlow from the *Aysgarth Falls*. A sheer falsity, Halfhyde had said. Higgins had agreed, still smiling, but had said that, false or not, the warrant would be executed if there was any trouble. Porteous Higgins had everything very well sewn up, even as far north as Rockhampton in Queensland. It had been obvious all along that the crews of the coasters had to be in his pocket; now it seemed that the Queensland police were also. With an ill grace, Halfhyde had been forced to accept his passengers.

He strode his bridge, face formidable, his mind racing. Higgins was there to watch over his cargo for himself, to ensure its arrival at its proper destination. The man was taking a big risk; his fiat could hardly run in England or Ireland as well as in Australia. Halfhyde must bide his time; but the voyage ahead was going to be one of immense strain. He would need to watch his temper among other things . . .

The speaking-tube whistled from his cabin. Surprised, he bent to answer it. 'Bridge. Who's that?'

'I, Captain.'

Higgins' voice. Halfhyde stiffened angrily. Before he could explode Higgins spoke again. 'Come down, Captain. I wish to speak to you.'

'I think you will come up here, Higgins.'

'No.' The tone was flat, brooking no argument. 'Privacy . . .

29

so important to you. I think you understand.' Below in the cabin, the plug was put back in the speaking-tube. Halfhyde, turning, met the eye of Perry, Officer of the Watch. Very briefly; then Perry looked away. It was clear he had overheard. Halfhyde fumed. What was going to be the effect on the ship's discipline now? He put the best face possible on it and told the First Mate, formally, that he would be in his cabin if required.

Then he went down the ladder.

Higgins was seated in Halfhyde's swivel chair, smoking a cigar. He waved Halfhyde to the other chair. 'Please sit down, Captain.'

'What the devil—'

'Please. Let us be civilized, Captain.' Porteous Higgins pointed his cigar towards the door to the master's deck. Halfhyde turned; Gaboon stood in the doorway, kneading his fingers as though preparing for an act of strangulation. Yellow teeth were bared over the underhung jaw as Gaboon grinned at him. He swung back towards Higgins.

He said harshly, 'I command this ship. No-one else does. Get up from my chair.'

Higgins looked at him, evidently read the message in his eyes, and shrugged, as much as to say, I have the whip hand and there's no need to stress it for the moment. He got to his feet, moved across to the vacant chair, and sat heavily in it. He waved his cigar nonchalantly at the swivel chair. 'Yours, Captain, if it means so much to you.'

Halfhyde remained standing, fists clenched, chest rising and falling to deep breaths of fury. 'What is it you wanted to say, Higgins?'

'Some words of warning. When do we reach Valparaiso?'

'Forty days.'

Higgins nodded. 'A long passage in a slow ship. The call is for stores and bunkers, I take it?'

'Yes. And cargo if any's to be found. I have space in my tween-decks.'

'You'll not take any cargo,' Higgins said.

'I'll do as I think fit, and I'll not ask your permission.'

'You haven't got it. You'll not take cargo, Captain. I want no

30

cargo loaded on top of my cases. In Valparaiso, you'll give no shore leave to your crew, and you'll not set foot ashore yourself. I concede that you'll have business to transact, but you'll not attend to it ashore yourself. I shall do that for you, acting as your agent. In short, there will be no contact with the shore except through myself. When you are dealing with your pilot, and the port authorities who will board in Valparaiso, Gaboon will be in attendance. I believe you understand. Gaboon will not hesitate . . . . I am playing for high stakes, Captain. The highest.'

'You mean Gaboon's your personal killer. He won't get away with that, in Valparaiso. If there's murder done, the ship'll be held. Then it'll be all up with you.'

Once again Porteous Higgins smiled. 'Well, we shall see. There are other ways. It need not come to murder . . . overt murder. Kindly open up your safe, Captain.'

Halfhyde stared. 'My safe?'

'Please.'

'What do you want with my safe, Higgins?'

'Shipmasters are permitted to be armed. Most masters keep a revolver in their safes. You are to be disarmed. Don't let us have any trouble, Captain.'

Halfhyde said, 'You'll keep your dirty hands out of my safe, Higgins. I—' He broke off; he had heard the soft pad of feet behind him. He turned sharply, but was too late. Long arms were wrapped around his body, pinning him completely. The grinning face of Gaboon was thrust close to his, the yellowed fangs bared, the breath foetid. Higgins got to his feet and came across, ran his fingers through Halfhyde's pockets, found the bunch of keys secured to a lanyard around the waist. Bringing out a pocket knife, whistling softly between his teeth, Porteous Higgins cut the lanyard and with the keys went over to the safe bolted to the bulkhead beside the roll-top desk. Finding the right key he swung the door open, saw the revolver lying on the bottom shelf, and removed it.

He turned back to Halfhyde. 'Effectively, I am now the master of this ship. You are the public figurehead – also, of course, the seagoing expert. Don't play me any tricks, Captain

Halfhyde. At the end of all this you will be well paid and if you are co-operative no harm will come to your ship. And in the meantime there's something else, some comfort,' he added with a salacious, oily smile. 'I'm not unaware of what has already taken place in this cabin. I've no objection to its continuance if it keeps you amenable.' He nodded at Gaboon. 'Let him go now.'

* * *

Pacing, pacing as that first day's sun went down the sky in a brilliant, spectacular sunset. Pacing the bridge still as the southern heavens filled with the luminescence of the myriad stars that hung like lamps above the silent sea and the streaming white wake of the ship. There was no sleep for Halfhyde; his very cabin had been sullied by the morning's presence of Porteous Higgins and Gaboon. The indignity would never cease to rankle, nor would its sequel. When released, Halfhyde had gone at once to his bridge and sent for Causton, the bosun. Hands, he said, had been laid upon his person; and Gaboon was to be held in arrest and locked into the fore peak. Four men would be necessary; and he would accompany the party himself. That had resulted in more indignity; guns had been produced and Halfhyde, unwilling to risk the lives of his crew, had been forced ignominiously to retreat. Higgins had been triumphant. 'Cool your temper, Captain,' he had advised. 'You might have expected this.'

Too true; Halfhyde recognized that a hot head had led him into it. And now matters were much worse: the whole crew would know that the master was under duress. By now the duress was overt: whenever Halfhyde went below either Higgins or Gaboon was in evidence, though they were keeping clear of the bridge. Watch succeeded watch: Perry, Foster, Perry again, Foster . . . the *Taronga Park* could not afford the luxury of a third mate, but Halfhyde intended to help out on a long passage by relieving decks to give his two watchkeepers a spell. He had spoken to Perry and Foster, taking them fully into his confidence now. Perry was somewhat withdrawn: the Captain hadn't behaved well in fobbing him off earlier.

32

Halfhyde made the point that he hadn't wished to involve his officers, preferring to take any subsequent trouble on his own shoulders. Now, he could no longer keep them out of it. What was to be done? Perry's suggestion was a concerted attack by the whole crew. Easy enough, he said. But Halfhyde still wouldn't risk unarmed men's lives against Higgins' guns. Not yet; a time might come, and it might come in Valparaiso with the pilot and port officials aboard.

Yet there was still the threat of Gaboon's presence while shore people were aboard. Higgins' henchman would be the safeguard all the way through. That was baffling in itself, though: surely, only a madman would produce a gun and threaten the master in front of the Chilean authorities?

And the girl, Victoria Penn?

Just a prostitute, really – but an attractive one. Strange, whatever she was, that Higgins should bring her aboard as comfort for a shipmaster who was, as it were, in irons. Irons of Higgins' own making. Why bother?

Dead tired, worrying nagging at his mind, Halfhyde went at last below. It was by now the morning watch, the four to eight; at any minute dawn would be stealing across from easterly, bringing its promise of the sun's tropical heat with not the faintest breeze to dispel it. Gaboon was walking up and down the master's deck outside the cabin ports. There was no sign of Porteous Higgins, who was probably asleep while Gaboon kept watch. Halfhyde went into his cabin and found Victoria Penn sitting, like Higgins earlier, in his chair.

She said, 'Hullo there.'

'Out,' Halfhyde said savagely.

She seemed hurt, wincing a little at his tone. 'Look, I—'

'Leave me alone. I need sleep. I don't know why you were brought aboard and I don't care.'

He turned towards his bunk. As he did so a shaft of dawn light struck through the port and lit the girl's face, and he saw the sparkle of tears and the look of hopelessness.

Let her cry: she was of the Higgins camp and he wanted none of that. She left the cabin. Dropping on to his bunk fully dressed, he was asleep in seconds.

33

* * *

He heard the sounds in the cabin and thought at first it might be the girl again but it wasn't; it was his steward, a small, wiry man named Butcher, bringing a cup of tea.

'Time?' Halfhyde demanded.

'Six bells, sir. In the forenoon watch, sir.'

Halfhyde grunted and sat up, still tired and with the beginnings of a headache. The day was hot, supremely so, and close to suffocating. Butcher coughed and said, 'There's a young lady, sir. The one what boarded—'

'Yes, yes, I know. Where is she?'

'Out on deck, sir. She asks for a word with you.'

'Very persistent. Where's Higgins, and Gaboon?'

'Mr 'Iggins is out there on your deck, sir. The other's turned in.'

Halfhyde nodded. Higgins and Gaboon were sharing a spare cabin, a double-berth one aft in the engineers' quarters. The girl had been allocated the only single berth, also aft. All the while he had been asleep Halfhyde's mind had been busy in nightmarish speculation about the future for himself and his ship, nightmares in which both Higgins and Gaboon swelled and swelled like balloons until they were laid totally about the ship, enveloping it like hideous, swollen jellyfish, bags of putrescence that he shot at with his revolver but which refused to burst. That, and the girl. That glimpse of a saddened, disappointed face was in his thoughts now. They'd had that night together, after all. Perhaps he had been harsh. But the situation was a remarkably curious one. Clearly the girl had some role to play, but what?

He said, 'All right. Send her in. Not right away, though. I'll wash first.'

'Yessir. Water's ready, sir.'

Halfhyde stripped, pulled on a dressing-gown, and left the cabin, crossing a short space of deck to his tiny bathroom at the side of the ship beneath the bridge wing. Higgins had gone; he saw Victoria on the other side of the deck, leaning on the rail and watching the sun's golden ride across the blue. Halfhyde

34

shaved and washed, went back to his cabin and dressed in a clean shirt and white trousers. Then he sent Butcher to tell the girl she could come in.

She came, smiling. 'Grouchiness all gone?' she asked.

'Partly. Would you mind telling me why you're here?'

'Porteous Higgins,' she said.

'That part I could guess. Why?'

'Couldn't leave me behind, that's all.'

'Too dangerous?'

She nodded. 'I know too much about him.'

'Tell me,' Halfhyde said.

'It wouldn't do any good. Don't press, please.'

He looked at her closely; there was strain in her eyes. 'All right,' he said. 'For now anyway, I won't. Just one thing. Are you his girl?' It wasn't likely in the circumstances, but he had to know for sure.

She said, 'No. Oh, no. I hate his guts.'

'But you sleep with him?'

'It's been known, not that he's very interested. That's not his line. He's dedicated to making money and gaining power where he can. He's powerful, all right.'

Halfhyde nodded. 'Why are you interested in me?' he asked.

'I went for you,' she said, 'the moment you came into the shop. My sort, I reckon. Don't know if you understand. Not that I'm worth it,' she added.

'Why not?'

She laughed; a sound he'd come to like. 'Need you ask? I'm not particularly ashamed of it, mind. It's one way of making a living. You've got to get by, haven't you?'

He didn't answer, but got up and went across to her, and put his hands on her shoulders. 'I've got a living to make, too. And I've got a ship to run. At this moment, I'm not really running it, even though there's no interference with the ship as such or with the bridge. I don't like not being in control.'

'No,' she said. 'You were Navy. I know the details. You were a bloody fool to get into this mess, weren't you?'

He said between his teeth, 'That has to be admitted. But I want to know the facts about Porteous Higgins.'

35

'I reckon you already know them. He's a twister. He's real crook.'

He released her shoulders and stood back. He went to the port and looked out. All ship-shape, the fo'c'sle hands going about their work on deck, but glancing, he saw, constantly towards the bridge. Everyone was on edge. Somehow he had to reassert his total authority. The girl probably couldn't help; she was in Higgins' power. Halfhyde said, 'I don't see where you fit. Tell me about yourself.'

She shrugged. 'Little enough to tell and what there is, isn't interesting.'

'Tell me all the same. For a start, I get the idea you're not Australian. The accent isn't what I'd call total.'

'True,' she said. 'I was born in Yorkshire, the North Riding.'

He turned to her. 'So was I. A farm in Wensleydale.'

'Near enough neighbours,' she said. 'Me, I was born on a farm, too. Keld, the other side of the Buttertubs Pass. About the same time as you, I reckon. But I never heard the name of Halfhyde.'

'Nor I yours.'

'I wasn't Penn then.'

'Married?'

She nodded. 'That's right. He died. He was a miner, over in Western Australia – Collie Creek. There was a roof fall and he never came out.'

'I'm sorry,' Halfhyde said. 'What was your maiden name?'

'I was born Paddlethwaite. Victoria Paddlethwaite, that was me.' She paused, then said with a touch of bravado, 'Reckon you could have heard *that* name.'

Halfhyde stared at her. He recalled the name, though in his youth it had been spoken in bated breath, and that rarely. It had never been mentioned in the Halfhyde home after the scandal had broken and shattered the good people of Wensleydale and Swaledale. Ben Paddlethwaite, a shepherd, a trusted man, had been caught in the act of rifling his master's desk before the farm wages were paid out. The farmer himself had found him with his hand in the gold half-sovereigns. Paddlethwaite, a rat caught in a trap, had turned on the farmer,

36

seized his neck, and strangled him. Paddlethwaite had then
disappeared but had been caught after six weeks, tried, and
sentenced to death. He had been hanged in York. Halfhyde had
been barely ten years old, the girl probably seven or eight.
Halfhyde had heard the details from his contemporaries on the
Wensleydale farms, boys who had picked it up from hearsay as
the shepherds gossiped at their work on the fells. Paddlethwaite's family had left the district and no more had been
heard of them.

He asked, 'Did you all come out to Australia?'

She shook her head. 'No. Mum and the rest of us, we had to
take to the roads. Just walked away from Keld . . . I reckon you
can't imagine what it was like. Like gipsies. There wasn't any
work. Not much food either. Bloody outcasts.'

'And it wasn't your fault. I think I can imagine some of it.
The bitterness. There's a lot of unfairness.'

'You bet,' she said. 'Well, we had to put up with it. As I said,
we walked. Ended up down in Liverpool. Then it was the
workhouse and all split up. Me, I was sent to an orphanage. I
never saw Mum or me brothers again. When I was fourteen I
ran away, went down to the docks, and stowed away aboard a
square-rigger. Under a tarpaulin in a lifeboat . . . I was bloody
near dead when they found me. Anyway, they carried me on to
Sydney, didn't put me ashore when we called on the way in –
Valparaiso, Iquique. I was put to work in a kind of way . . . if
you follow my meaning. They didn't want to lose me, see. Not
so often you get a girl of my sort loose aboard a windjammer. In
Sydney, I buggered off and found a bloke in the Cross who paid
me way for a bit, then he dropped me. Then I met Harry Penn
and he was daft enough to marry me.'

'How long were you married?'

She said, 'Four years, just about.'

'And after Harry was killed?'

'Came back from Collie Creek, back to where I knew – the
Cross. Then I got in Higgins' net. He wanted a girl in the
bloody shop . . . and sometimes, like I said, other things. I
hadn't much choice. Bloody Higgins had found out a lot about
me and he had a hold. Prostitution, stowing away . . . they'd

have deported me back to England. Besides, Higgins was a sort of security, money and a roof over me head.'

'You knew he wasn't straight?'

'Like a corkscrew,' she said. 'Yes, I knew. I knew the Cross pretty well, after all.'

'Tell me one thing,' Halfhyde said quietly, looking into the dark eyes. 'Why does Higgins let you talk to me? Why did he bring you aboard, so you could tell me about him?'

'I told you, didn't I? I'm too dangerous to leave behind.'

He said, 'That doesn't answer the question, does it? He's put no barriers between you and me. Rather the opposite.'

She looked back at him as though he were a child, a child who needed to have his innocence shattered. She said, 'Jesus, Captain, you aren't going to do any talking about Porteous bloody Higgins. You're going nowhere, not if Higgins has his way. You crossed him, right? Now you're for the high jump, long before we make anywhere you can talk to the law.'

He laughed. 'Higgins won't get the chance. When the showdown comes, I have a crew – he hasn't.'

'That,' the girl said, 'is what you think, Captain. Look, your fo'c'sle is about three quarters full of blokes who've taken gold from Higgins. Once he got the word you were signing all old Jakey Good's crew, he knew just who to approach, right?'

FOUR

The girl couldn't name any names; Halfhyde, who had suspected, back in Sydney, a possible suborning of his crew, would have to find out the identities of the disaffected men for himself. Their attitudes might give a clue in time. It turned out on further questioning that Porteous Higgins hadn't taken the girl into his confidence and her information had been gleaned from scraps of overheard conversation, some of it being in fact no more than deduction. So Porteous Higgins wouldn't know that Victoria had told him about the bought fo'c'sle hands. That gave Halfhyde some sort of advantage. Also, in part it explained why Higgins was allowing them to be together; but there was still a lot of that aspect yet to be unravelled. It didn't appear to be in Higgins' character to bring any sort of comfort – to use Higgins' own word – to an enemy. Halfhyde's mind roved this way and that, seeking light. If most of his crew were against him, his chances were poor. Both Higgins and Gaboon were armed; members of the crew, for all Halfhyde knew, could also be armed from the cargo. Higgins could by now have made his way into the holds from the tween-decks. For Halfhyde to attempt to broach the cargo for his own use would obviously be impossible: he would have insufficient control for that in view of his ignorance as to who was for him and who against; and in any case that would be the one thing above all that Porteous Higgins would be watching out for. As matters stood Higgins could seize the ship whenever it suited him, and force Halfhyde and his officers to obey his orders. And Halfhyde himself, after that –and Perry, and Foster, and Baird? Once the ship was berthed in Queenstown, then, at the latest, their usefulness would be over. It wasn't difficult to dispose of bodies, even if they had to be taken out to sea on a dark night and dumped from one of the ship's boats. It had been done before.

Halfhyde paced the cabin, watched by the girl. He read the concern in her face. Watching him, she said almost diffidently, 'Me, I'll root for you. I'm on your side.'

'And me on yours,' he said. 'I take it you want to be free of Higgins?'

She nodded. 'That's dead right, I do.'

'Back in England?'

'I don't know,' she said. 'I've got to like Australia in spite of it all. I could go back . . . as your cabin girl, right?'

He smiled. 'I dare say it could be arranged.' The total incongruity struck him forcibly. In this cabin he had already lain with the girl, had responded vigorously to her. If his parents on the farm in Wensleydale could know how a Paddlethwaite had entered his life . . . if Sir John and Lady Willard could but know of that night . . . and Mildred! He gave a sudden laugh; Mildred would have one attack of the vapours hard on the heels of the other. This girl was everything Mildred was not: common, promiscuous and vital. She was alive. Her body was made, as Mildred's was not, for union with a man. She would never forgo bed for a horse-race.

She asked, 'What are you going to do about Higgins?'

'I don't know yet,' he said. 'I've a few people I can take into my confidence, men I know I can trust. A scheme will be worked out. You can be sure of that.'

She grinned up at him, the grin making her look more abandoned. It was an urchin's grin. He liked it. She asked, 'Going to win out, are we?'

He liked the 'we' as well. 'We're going to win out,' he said gravely. He bent and took her in his arms for a moment, ruffling her hair, then kissed her on the mouth. 'Off you go for now.'

'You sure you don't want—'

'Quite sure. I've things to do now.'

* * *

40

He sent for the First Mate. He told Perry most of what the girl had said. Perry gave a concerned whistle, said he'd be keeping a close eye on the fo'c'sle hands; it wouldn't take him long to make some assessment of who was against the ship and who could be trusted. He'd had a long experience of seamen and reckoned he was a fair judge. And he would pass the word discreetly to Foster. 'How about Causton, sir?' he asked.

Halfhyde said, 'Not for now. Later perhaps. Not that I don't trust Causton—'

'He's all right,' Perry said. 'Sailed with me and Captain Good a long while. I'd trust him anywhere.'

'So would I, Mr Perry, but something could leak – just by the way he might treat the men with that knowledge in his mind. I'm not taking the risk at this stage. Causton could be too loyal, and it would show. Everything depends on Higgins not getting to know what *we* know.'

Perry nodded. 'I see the point, Captain.' He glanced up at the port, then lifted his eyebrows at Halfhyde. Halfhyde nodded; he, too, had noted the passing hairy form of Gaboon, out there on the master's deck. Gaboon, the man of silence – he hadn't spoken to anyone aboard.

'That's all, Mr Perry, thank you,' he said in a loud voice.

'Yes, sir.' Perry got to his feet. As he lifted towards Halfhyde he whispered, 'How about Baird, sir? You going to—'

'Shortly, yes. A decent interval so as not to arouse suspicions of a conference . . . and the good Baird won't be easy. I feel it in my bones.'

* * *

Baird wasn't easy; he never was, never had been according to Perry. When, later that day, Halfhyde sent a message asking the Chief Engineer if he would be so good as to come up to his cabin, Baird looked lugubrious and dour, suspecting some aspersions to be cast upon his engine-room and its complement.

'You'll take a drink, Chief?' Halfhyde asked.

'Aye. Whisky.'

'What else indeed?' Halfhyde gestured to his steward.

41

Butcher poured two whiskies, adding a little water to Half-hyde's. The Chief Engineer took his whisky neat.

'Your health, Captain.'

'And yours, Mr Baird. All right, Butcher, that'll be all.'

'Yessir.' Butcher left the cabin; he could be trusted, Halfhyde was sure of that since Higgins had wanted him replaced by Gaboon, but there was nothing to be gained by letting the information spread.

'What did ye want to see me about?' Baird asked forbearing-ly. 'Some unfounded complaint I don't doubt. The deck people are all the same. No offence, of course, Captain.'

'None taken. I appreciate the problem of engineers—'

'Hah!'

Halfhyde waved a hand amiably. 'Well, believe me or not, just as you like. There's no complaint. There's something far more serious.'

'Oh, aye.'

'And it's between you and me – very strictly. I must impress that upon you – you'll understand why in a moment. You and me, Perry and Foster. No-one else at this stage.'

'Uh-huh.' Mr Baird knocked back the remainder of his whisky, then put the glass down hard on Halfhyde's desk and looked meaningfully at the Captain. Halfhyde reached for the bottle, pouring a larger measure this time, still no water.

'Thank you,' Baird said. 'Ye're more generous than yon Butcher makes you seem, Captain.'

'I trust I'm a reasonably generous man. Currently I'm a worried one. I seek your help, Mr Baird.'

'Oh, aye.' The tone was indifference itself.

Halfhyde, feeling irritated, took a deep breath and told the Chief Engineer as much as he had told Perry. Baird looked incredulous. 'All my eye and Betty Martin,' he said with scorn. 'By the holy God, the deck people'll believe anything!'

'Come now, Chief. You'll have seen for yourself the way Higgins and his tame gorilla came aboard—'

'Och, I hold no brief for yon monster. He has the look of being straight from the jungle, has Gaboon. But the story's too tall for me to give any credence to it. It's a kind of piracy you're suggesting, Captain.'

'You've done your time on the Australian coast. Surely you've heard tales about Porteous Higgins?'

'Aye, I have.'

'There you are then. Doesn't it tie up?'

Baird lifted his head and scratched reflectively beneath his chin. 'Ye're going beyond what ties up. Ye're talking of murder if I hear you right.'

'Murder and gun-running to potential Irish rebels – yes.'

'Fenians and all! The Clan-na-Gael, dyed in blood?'

Halfhyde nodded. 'Yes. Nothing less, I believe.'

'It's fantasy. Sheer fantasy! You have no proof about the cargo.'

'No proof that I can offer before a lot of us are dead,' Halfhyde agreed, beginning to wish he could murder his Chief Engineer. 'But all the proof *I* need—'

'Obtained from where? I'll tell you, Captain.' Mr Baird lifted his glass-free hand and pointed a finger at Halfhyde. 'From a loose woman, a prostitute from the Cross forbye, a wicked slut that it's a sin should have sat in the same cabin as a God-fearing Presbyterian, which I am and will be to my dying day. Lord, lord! Ye canna believe the word o' such a female, Captain, and I'll have none of it, none of it at all.'

The glass was emptied again. 'Another whisky?' Halfhyde snapped. 'Or will you have none of that either – as a God-fearing Presbyterian?'

'The two things are quite different.' Baird held out his glass. 'I think the female has had an effect on your mind, Captain. Time will tell if the effect upon your body is the same. No, no.' He held up a hand as Halfhyde began to react angrily. 'The devil does his work upon the weak, Captain. That is written in the Good Book for all to read if they wish. I—'

'I'm not talking about the devil, Mr Baird. I'm talking about Porteous Higgins, which may well be the same thing but is currently more immediate and dangerous. I'll thank you to stop casting doubts upon my sanity and pay proper attention to your Captain and owner—'

'Ah!' Baird said triumphantly. 'Here's the threat emerging

43

now.'

'It is not. It will emerge if you persist in being an ostrich, but not until then. Now, Mr Baird. I said I sought your help. It's not too much to ask.'

'What, precisely, are you asking, Captain?'

'I don't know yet. It's early days. But I may need the co-operation of the engine-room . . . and I'll want to know who's loyal amongst your firemen and greasers and who's not.'

'They're a rat-bag collection o' pure rubbish,' Baird said, 'mostly.'

'Sort them out, then. Be sure which is which. That's all I ask for now. And keep your eyes and ears open.'

Once again Baird scratched his chin. Halfhyde believed something had penetrated. Baird was indeed thinking that the new master had a somewhat wild and rangy look, and a temper very near the surface, and had been in the Queen's ships to boot, which was almost a guarantee of insanity in his view – yet in spite of all this, Baird saw that Halfhyde did in fact believe what he had been saying. And there was no doubt at all that the man Higgins had a sordid reputation and Baird had been displeased to see him come aboard off the Barrier Reef. There might be something in all this, perhaps.

Baird said, 'You told me, I think, that Higgins means to use you to get his cargo just where he wants it.'

'Yes.'

'In that case, you have plenty of time. He'll not strike at Valparaiso. Higgins is no seaman. We'll all be necessary to him until the end. The very end. That's if all this is to be believed at all, of course. I'll take another wee dram, Captain, then I must be away below.'

Out was thrust the glass; Halfhyde poured again. He said, 'To repeat myself, all this is between those few of us I spoke of. Nothing is to be said beyond this cabin, not even to your Second Engineer. Nothing. You may doubt my sanity—'

'Aye . . .'

'But you'll keep it to yourself. I believe you understand me, Mr Baird?'

Baird's breath hissed through his teeth. He knew that chief

44

engineers could be signed off at the master's whim in the United Kingdom with no return passage to Australia; and Baird's home these days was in Sydney. Looking angry, Baird left the cabin.

* * *

Slowly, as the *Taronga Park* steamed easterly on passage for Valparaiso, the atmosphere in the ship worsened. Either Higgins or Gaboon was constantly in evidence about the decks; the bosun, Causton, made a complaint to the First Mate.

'They're getting in the way of the hands, sir, working about the ship. If you ask me, they're snooping . . . but don't ask me why 'cos I don't know. Unless they don't trust us with their bloody cargo.'

Perry gave him a sharp look: Halfhyde hadn't wanted anything about the cargo's true nature to leak to the crew. 'Why d'you say that, Causton?'

The bosun shrugged. 'Don't say I do, Mister. But those buggers . . .'

Perry made light of it. 'Crosses to be borne. Passengers help to pay the ship's way – and your wages, and mine.'

Causton gave him a sour look, and spat skilfully over the rail to leeward. 'Funny passengers! Funny way to come aboard an' all. Captain Good, he'd never have allowed it. Never.'

'Nothing to be done about it now. You know that.'

'Yes,' Causton agreed doubtfully, 'I reckon you're right at that, Mr Perry. But I see trouble ahead . . . specially with that Gaboon. What is he, d'you know – an abo?'

Perry shrugged. 'I've no idea. The name could be, I suppose, but he doesn't look like an abo.'

'I reckon I've come across the name before, sir. Not sure . . . but there was a murder up Brisbane way, more'n ten, eleven years ago now. Made quite a splash. I don't know . . . it could have been Gaboon.'

Perry said, 'If it was, he obviously didn't swing for it!'

'No, that's right. Found not guilty. There was talk afterwards of a nobbled jury, not in the bloody newspapers, of course, but I remember picking up some yarns in Brisbane soon

45

after. No-one else was ever charged not that I ever heard.'

'What sort of murder was it?'

'Bloody nasty. An abo woman, raped first. Then the killer, he'd gone mad, must have – the woman had been cut to pieces. Bits here and there – legs, arms, torso – you know the sort of thing.'

Perry nodded. 'Yes, I remember hearing about it now. I was in a square-rigger out of Liverpool in those days, one of Iredale and Porter's. Heard about it in Sydney. I don't tie up the name Gaboon with it, though.' He looked ahead across the Pacific; the water lay calm still, almost like a pond. No wind at all. Too calm, and a curious stillness in the atmosphere. An utter silence, broken only by the racket from the engine and the sound of the sea washing down the ship's sides. Perry said, 'Do you feel it, Causton?'

Causton understood. There was a shift of weather imminent. 'Aye, sir. Soon we'll see the line of cloud.'

'Start securing for a blow,' Perry said. 'Steel-wire strops on the anchors, storm covers on the hatches and extra battens too. And lifelines fore and aft. I'll have a word with the Captain.' He lifted an eyebrow at the bosun. 'If I were you, I'd not bother to use any particular precautions if Higgins or Gaboon ventures on deck after it starts! I don't like them any more than you do, and that's a fact.'

Causton went about his deck duties, shouting for the hands, and Perry climbed to the Captain's cabin. Halfhyde, who had also studied the sky, had been about to send for him and now approved the orders given for securing the ship against foul weather. Perry reported his conversation with the bosun. Halfhyde had no knowledge of the Brisbane murder; but he agreed with Perry that if the killer had been Gaboon, and if there had been a nobbled jury, then it was likely enough that Higgins had done the nobbling and had then taken Gaboon into his net for future use.

'Conjecture,' Halfhyde said, 'but it might fit. Though I don't know if it's any help to us now. We know already that they're a couple of twisters.'

'Rape, sir,' Perry said remindingly.

46

'Meaning?'

Perry said, 'There's the woman who embarked.'

'Yes. You may be sure I shall watch out, Mr Perry. You may be very sure of that. But I doubt if he'd take the risk. Higgins won't want any spanners in the works.' Halfhyde looked out of his port, then turned back to the First Mate. 'The horizon's darkening fast, Mr Perry. Call all hands. I shall be on the bridge.'

Perry left the cabin and went fast down the ladders to the after well-deck. Halfhyde climbed to the bridge, where Foster was on watch. There was a long, low line of heavy cloud ahead, cloud that was already extending, reaching out towards the *Taronga Park* with hastening fingers, and the sea between the ship and the horizon was already ruffled by an increasing wind and pock-marked with the lash of rain. Looking aft, Halfhyde saw Porteous Higgins emerge from the door into the engineers' alleyway, accompanied by Gaboon. There was a short conversation, then Gaboon went back into the engineers' accommodation. Higgins came forward, lurching a little as the *Taronga Park* began to roll to the suddenly disturbed Pacific.

FIVE

Higgins appeared at the head of the bridge ladder. He asked, 'Is it bad weather?'

'Use your eyes,' Halfhyde said curtly.

Higgins' heavy face flushed. 'Will it delay us?'

'Yes, without a doubt. I shall have to reduce speed.'

'It can be made up afterwards.'

'On the contrary, it cannot. I have not the extra knots in hand.'

'Look,' Higgins said, moving forward, his face ugly. 'It's got to be made up, right?'

Halfhyde faced him squarely. 'What you're saying is, you want to arrive in Queenstown on the given date. You're not likely to. The sea's the sea, and the *Taronga Park* is no liner with a fixed schedule to be kept to. I shall not punish my engines. The ship will make her landfall when I say so, and at this moment I'm in no position to say anything about that. As you should have known from the start, Higgins. Mine isn't the first cargo you've shipped – and you must have shipped cargoes in sail before now, with all a windjammer's irregularity.'

'Steam's steam, Halfhyde. You can do it if you try, and I'm not concerned about your engines. I want to speak to your Chief Engineer.'

'My Chief Engineer takes his orders from me.'

'We'll see about that. Send for him.'

Halfhyde's jaw was thrust out and his lips were tight. 'I shall do no such thing. Mr Baird is needed on the starting platform below.'

48

'I said—'

'I'm aware of what you said, Higgins. My answer stands. And now get off my bridge.'

'I shall not—'

'You will obey orders, and immediately.' Halfhyde seized the heavy body, slewed it round, getting a lock on the arms as he drew them up behind, and propelled Porteous Higgins to the head of the ladder. Then he released the arms and gave the man a shove. Higgins went down the ladder out of control, bumping hard on the treads and landing in a heap at the bottom. He was beside himself with fury. A fist was shaken up towards Halfhyde, but he didn't come back up the ladder. Instead he went aft; Halfhyde's guess was that he was bound for the engine-room. Halfhyde grinned to himself as he turned his attention back to his ship: Baird could be relied upon to give Porteous Higgins very short shrift – and might at the same time be convinced at last of Halfhyde's total sanity . . .

* * *

The rain came down in solid sheets; the men on the bridge were soaked to the skin within seconds of the storm striking; water ran down the collars of their oilskins, ran up the sleeves when an arm was raised. The *Taronga Park* rolled violently, and pitched at the same time. The plates shuddered to the impact of the waves, wind-blown waves that at times topped the ship, rearing like the sides of mountains, rearing up to come down in heavy masses that drummed on the deck and the cargo hatches as they landed, then swilled about the ship like a river, overwhelming the washports and submerging men to their waists. It had come with such speed that the battening-down of the ship had not yet been completed and the hands were still working on the exposed decks. Halfhyde, not yet knowing his ship's capabilities in filthy weather, was a worried man. The safety of his crew was his first consideration, but he had all to lose beyond that: his home and his livelihood. Many a ship had gone without trace over the years in the sudden South Pacific storms that ravaged the islands in their tracks. Nature was still stronger than man or man's artefacts. The seas were one of nature's most malignant agents when nature so desired.

This time, it seemed as though nature was in a bad mood.

Halfhyde watched from the bridge as the First Mate battled with the hands to rig the storm cover over the fore hatch. The wind tore and ripped, seizing the canvas from men's hands, bringing out the finger-nails as it did so. Perry was shouting into the wind, was everywhere at once, an excellent First Mate leading his hands rather than merely driving them. Then Halfhyde saw the lift of the starboard for'ard corner of the fair-weather hatch canvas. He took up his megaphone.

'Mr Perry! Starboard fore corner! It's going!'

Perry heard, looked, took a couple of seamen with him and ran across, lurching heavily to the ship's roll as the sea sent her over to port. He had virtually to climb a hill . . . and he was just too late. The cover lifted further and then tore back, coming clear altogether of its chocks and flailing away into a sky nearly as dark as night. In the same moment a heavy sea dropped aboard with smashing force, taking the fore hatch fair and square. Perry and the hands vanished in swirling foam, emerged looking like drowned rats clinging for their lives to whatever offered a hand-hold.

Halfhyde watched in horror.

The hatch planks themselves had lifted. Water cascaded down. The deck was a shambles. The foul-weather cover had been taken by the wind to wrap itself around the foot of the foremast and was flailing about like a sail ripped from the cringles. As Halfhyde watched one of the hatch planks was taken by the roaring wind. It flew across the deck, fast and heavy, and took one of the fo'c'sle hands full in the face. The man fell back streaming blood and shattered bone, took the guardrail hard with his back, gave one scream that tore right through the high note of the wind, then flopped formlessly overboard into the wild water. Seconds later the body was seen to be lifted high by a gigantic wave, a wave that rose higher than its predecessors, well above the level of the bridge, carrying the man with it and then falling suddenly away to drop him like a sack of potatoes across the fo'c'sle head, where he came down to thump cruelly across the iron of one of the cable clenches. No man could have lived through that; Halfhyde believed the man's back had been broken already, when he had been hurled against the guardrail. The First Mate, however, was lurching for the ladder to the fo'c'sle head when the remains were thankfully removed by another sea.

Halfhyde found sweat mixing with the water that had seeped through his oilskin. He lifted his megaphone again. 'Mr Perry, the tween-deck!'

Perry waved an acknowledgement. Halfhyde watched him go below. Perry would cope, if anyone could. His own place was on the bridge, the one place from which he could anticipate the next emergency, the one place from where he might be able to save his ship. All the while he had another anxiety, an anxiety brought about by his talk with Perry before the storm had struck: the girl, Victoria Penn. Gaboon had gone aft into the engineers' alleyway where her cabin was, and he had not come back. Rape was filling all of Halfhyde's mind that was not concerned with his ship. Gaboon was no-one's idea of a bedmate.

He tried to be dispassionate. She was, or had been, a prostitute.

* * *

The storm lasted twenty-four hours. When it had passed, a heavy swell was left and the skies were grey. There was a horrible clamminess in the air and it was close to the point of suffocation below decks and in the engine spaces. No further damage had been done and the pumps had coped with the inflow to the fore hold; the *Taronga Park* was only slightly down by the head now and would soon be riding to her proper trim. A certain amount of water damage was found in the hold but this was not as bad as it might have been. The hatch planking had been quickly replaced during the storm and the cover backed up with extra tarpaulins that had kept out further water. During the subsequent inspection of the hold Perry had been under Higgins' gun; no chance at all of getting his hands on any of the cargo.

When it was safe to do so, Halfhyde left the bridge for his

cabin and some rest. Before he had got his soaked clothing off, he was visited by the Chief Engineer. Baird had already reported by voice-pipe to the bridge that all was well in the engine-room although there had been a number of occasions, felt by Halfhyde as the shudder had run through the ship, when the screw had lifted clear of the sea on the pitch and had raced badly, never a good thing for the main shaft.

Baird, however, had something else on his mind now and Halfhyde guessed what it was.

'Higgins,' Baird said.

'I know. How did you get on with him?'

'I do not,' Baird answered, 'appreciate interference.'

'Quite.'

'I told him so, in words in frequent use on Clydeside. The lads o' Greenock and the shipyards up river have a term for such as Higgins, one I'll not repeat in your cabin, Captain.'

Halfhyde gave an ironic bow, his eyes glimmering with the desire to laugh. 'And what did he do, Chief?'

'He buggered off,' Baird said unexpectedly and with scant thought for the Presbyterian Church of Scotland, 'with a big greaser behind him carrying a spanner, just in case he changed his mind and came back. Now, I don't like the man, nor Gaboon either, but I'm thinking, Captain, that if what you said was the truth, then Higgins would not have been chased away by a spanner. He'd have threatened with a gun – he was very anxious that I should mistreat my engines in his interest but he didn't exactly back his threats wi' action.'

Baird looked at Halfhyde with deep suspicion. 'I still think it's the result of a deranged mind,' he said sourly. 'The man's just an arrogant pusher but he'll never scare me and never mind his reputation. Now, I believe a whisky's been earned, Captain. What do you say?'

Forbearing to call for his steward, Halfhyde brought out the bottle himself. 'It's too early in the day for me, but I know the Scots take it for breakfast if not before.'

'Slander,' Baird said.

Halfhyde poured a generous measure then asked if the Chief Engineer had heard of any trouble in the engineers' alleyway.

'No trouble,' Baird said. 'What sort o' trouble had you in mind, Captain?'

'So long as there hasn't been any, it's not important.' Halfhyde knew that any mention of the girl would bring out all Baird's Presbyterian instincts and would induce a sermon on women who were no better than they should be, women who asked for what they got, women that no decent man should have any truck with. He didn't wish to hear it. The whisky was quickly consumed and Baird left the cabin. Halfhyde completed his undressing, now with the assistance of Butcher, then dropped on to his bunk. He was quickly asleep, overcome with sheer physical exhaustion. When he woke it was night; a bright moon shone through the port and the ship steamed placidly through a calm sea.

Halfhyde sat up, yawning, stretching his limbs. He looked through the port at the star-filled sky: impossible now to believe the chaos that his ship had so recently come through. The Pacific had many moods, many quick changes. The life of a seaman was at least varied.

Outside the port, a little to the starboard side of it, loomed Gaboon, thick and squat. Gaboon, on watch no doubt. His voice heavy with irony, Halfhyde, putting his head through the port, said, 'Good evening.'

No answer. To Halfhyde's recollection, Gaboon had not been known to utter aboard the *Taronga Park*. The strong, silent man ... Halfhyde felt immense irritation at surly uncommunicativeness. That was part of his Naval training: senior officers expected immediate answers; anything less was insolence. He snapped through the port, 'Have you not a tongue in your head, Gaboon? One would at least expect civility.'

Gaboon turned towards him, the hairy face thrusting close to the port and clearly visible in the moon. He opened his mouth wide, raised a hand and pointed down his throat. Broken teeth showed, blackened stumps in the light of the moon. The mouth was like an empty cavern: a root swelled and retreated at the back of it. No tongue. Gaboon was dumb.

Halfhyde felt nauseated. Higgins' work? It was probable that

Gaboon could neither read nor write. If also he couldn't speak, secrets would be safe with him. Gaboon's assets lay in that and in the colossal strength of his long arms.

Gaboon turned away, walked along the master's deck. Halfhyde could feel the man's presence still when there was a knock at his door. 'Come in,' he called. It was Victoria Penn.

'Sleep well?' she asked.

He nodded. 'Is everything all right with you?'

'I reckon so. Why?'

He said, 'Gaboon.' He reached up and shut the glass of the port, then brought the heavy iron deadlight down over it as well. Gaboon was nicely shut out. 'Before the storm hit, I saw him going into the engineers' alleyway.'

'Where his cabin is, you know that. Worried, were you?'

'Yes,' he answered.

She sat on the bunk. 'Don't be. Higgins has warned him off. He'll take note of that. Besides, I can take care of myself. Shown how a long while ago, by an old biddy down the Cross. Hatpin. Does a lot of damage.'

He reached out a hand to her; she took it. That night, she didn't leave the cabin.

* * *

The weeks were passing. Halfhyde paced the bridge, once again in deep thought. In the terms used aboard the windjammers on passage from the Cape of Good Hope to the Leeuwin, he was running his easting down fast. Valparaiso was his next problem and it would be coming up not long hence. It would need much luck, but there was the chance that at Valparaiso he could outwit Porteous Higgins and be free of the menace that dogged his ship. If only he could find the way: in days past, when difficulties had faced him aboard the Queen's ships, and in the *Aysgarth Falls* in this same part of the world's oceans, he had seldom been lost for some stratagem by which to bring trouble to an end. This time there was nothing: mostly, Higgins and Gaboon took pains not to be together; this meant that, since each was armed, one was always available to cover the other. Between them they had a stranglehold on the ship. In

54

reserve, as it were, they had the suborned members of Halfhyde's crew. So far there had been no signs as to which those men might be, though between them Halfhyde and his First Mate had some suspicions that might or might not prove accurate when the time came. But the current uncertainty precluded any arranged and concerted attack by the crew on Porteous Higgins.

Halfhyde pondered on Victoria Penn. She was an ally; there was still the mystery as to why Higgins had never interfered with her comings and goings, the nights they had passed together since that first experience. And Gaboon . . . the night the girl had come to him after he had slept away the weariness of the storm, he had asked her if she knew Gaboon was dumb. She had not known; she had never seen Gaboon until she and Higgins had been joined by him in Rockhampton for the passage out to the *Taronga Park* aboard the coasters. She had wondered at Gaboon's total silence and that was all. She didn't know if he'd been connected with the ten-year-old murder of the abo woman in Brisbane.

She was not, in fact, much help; not yet. But Halfhyde had believed her when she had said she wanted to be free of Porteous Higgins. It had held the ring of sincerity. He was immensely sorry for the girl; she hadn't had much of a life. He would do his best for her. That, he swore to himself. She was still young, with a better life somewhere ahead. There was a whimsicality in her face that made a strong appeal . . . he caught himself up sharply. Help her he would, but he must not let his emotions become involved. He was, all said and done, in the eyes of God a married man: a man by his own rashness married to a block of ice, as fixed to Mildred as a prehistoric mammoth entombed in a glacier. Sympathy, pity was as far as it must go. Or perhaps a mistress, to be supported along with his obligations to Mildred? Halfhyde smiled to himself bitterly. Until his shipping venture made some money he could scarcely afford one woman, let alone two.

Pacing beneath the sun's brilliance, Halfhyde recalled a conversation he had had with his father, that solidly sensible Yorkshire farmer. One early morning they had taken the pony

55

and trap along the narrow twisting road that ran from Hawes in Upper Wensleydale across to Clapham on the western side of the Pennines and then had made the long climb up to the great mouth of Gaping Ghyll near the summit of Ingleborough. Halfhyde, then twenty and a midshipman in the British fleet, had broached the subject of marriage. In the manner of young officers, he had become enamoured of a barmaid blonde and beautiful in a public house in Portsmouth's Commercial Road. His father had grunted and said little beyond remarking that twenty was an unconscionably early age for any man to think of saddling himself with a wife; then he had added something that had stuck in Halfhyde's mind ever since.

'A penny,' his father had said, 'costs twopence once you're married. Think on it, boy.'

A mistress and a wife . . . that turned the penny into a total cost of threepence. Yet the temptation was strong. She was a frail woman, and undoubtedly fond of him; equally without doubt she was relying on him to steer her life on to a proper course. A kept woman until she found a man to marry . . . impatiently Halfhyde thrust her from his mind. The concentration must be upon Higgins and Gaboon.

Gaboon was on his silent watch again; Halfhyde, looking down from the bridge, saw him standing by the funnel casing above the boiler-room where the firemen toiled ceaselessly at their shovels, hurling the coal into the glowing furnaces, sweat-streaked, blackened men in dirty singlets and once-white duck trousers. If only the casing would give way beneath that monstrous man . . . but providence didn't behave that way.

Then, as Halfhyde watched from behind the cover of a bell-mouthed ventilator situated just aft of the bridge, something disturbing happened: Gaboon moved away aft past the opened engine-room skylight and down the ladder leading to the after well-deck. He vanished temporarily from Halfhyde's field of vision; and Halfhyde saw Victoria Penn come across from the port side and enter the engineers' alleyway on the starboard side.

A moment later he saw Gaboon again, now moving slowly aft along the deck, padding like an animal intent upon its prey, and go into the alleyway behind her. There was something in the hairy man's walk that started alarm bells sounding in Halfhyde's head. Porteous Higgins might have issued a warning; but basic instincts could cast warnings aside. Halfhyde turned to the First Mate.

'I'm going aft, Mr Perry. Aft, to the engineers' accommodation. Send down for the bosun to lay aft at once and join me.'

He went down the ladder fast.

SIX

'It's all right,' the girl said. She was pale but composed.
Halfhyde together with Causton had entered her cabin un-
ceremoniously and found Gaboon making heavy grunting
noises of pain and nursing a thigh. Victoria held up the hatpin.
'I told you,' she said. 'I can look after myself. The bugger won't
try that again. Reckon I just missed something vital.'

'Well,' Halfhyde said grimly, 'that does it. Gaboon's going
to the fore peak. Causton—'

There was a sound in the cabin doorway; Halfhyde swung
round. An angry Higgins stood there, a revolver in his hand.
'What's going on?' he demanded.

Halfhyde told him. Higgins said, 'One thing: Gaboon's not
going to any fore peak. Anyone who tries that will get a bullet.
I'll deal with him myself. Come out into the alleyway, Gaboon.'

There was fear in Gaboon's face now. He made a whining
sound, horrible to hear, but he obeyed Higgins. As Gaboon
moved to the door, Higgins stepped aside, lifted his revolver,
and rammed the barrel hard into Gaboon's mouth. Blood
spurted and there was a sound of breaking bone. Tears
streamed down Gaboon's face, matting the hair. Higgins,
thrusting with the revolver, pushed him back against the
bulkhead, withdrew the barrel, then brought it smashing into
the face, twice, first one side then the other. A roaring noise
came from Gaboon's broken lips 'Now get out,' Higgins said.

Gaboon fled.

'He won't do it a second time,' Higgins said flatly.

'I'm not taking the risk.' Halfhyde met the bosun's eye,

58

jerked his head fractionally towards Higgins. They both moved together. Causton got an arm around Higgins' neck, Halfhyde grabbed the hand that held the gun, forcing it down. There was an explosion that filled the small cabin with the stench of gunpowder and a bullet zipped past Halfhyde's leg into the woodwork of the bunk. Then the gun was free. Halfhyde aimed it at Porteous Higgins, breathing hard, face like ice. Staring Higgins in the eyes he spoke to the bosun.

'All right, Causton, I'll look after this end. Rouse out the hands and get Gaboon. Remember he's armed.'

'Aye, aye, sir.' Causton moved away for'ard at the double. By this time some men had gathered in the alleyway, the Chief Engineer among them.

Baird said, 'I heard a shot—'

'Right, Chief, you did. I want some of your firemen to take Higgins over. See to it, please.'

'It's a rum carry on.'

'Never mind about that, I'll explain later.'

'My firemen—'

'It was an order, Mr Baird. Kindly obey it at once.

Baird looked murderous but turned away. Halfhyde kept the revolver steady. Higgins, tight-lipped, said nothing but was very watchful. He seemed unworried. Halfhyde realized that the next few minutes would show who was for the ship and her master, who was for Higgins. That in itself would be a useful exercise. Meanwhile the ship was his again. He pushed the revolver into Higgins' stomach. 'On deck,' he said. 'As soon as I have hands here, you'll go into the fore peak with Gaboon. Move!'

Higgins turned slowly for the door and went out into the alleyway. Baird was seen coming along from the after end with three of his firemen. Halfhyde propelled Higgins out into the after well-deck, then he saw the bosun coming aft at the run but being overtaken by half a dozen hands from the fo'c'sle, all of them clutching belaying-pins. More were coming in behind, similarly armed. They closed in on the outnumbered group in the well-deck and were joined by two of Baird's firemen. The last thing Halfhyde was aware of was a seaman named Leary

59

coming for him with his belaying-pin, then he was struck hard on the head and went down cold on the deck.

* * *

He came to in his cabin, lying on the bunk. The girl was there, bathing his head with cold water. Perry was with her, looking anxiously at the Captain. Halfhyde tried to sit up. Sickness hit him, and a blinding headache. He shut his eyes; that was worse. The cabin spun around him, and moved up and down at the same time. He retched.

He heard Victoria saying. 'It's all right. I—'

Halfhyde interrupted in a weak voice. 'Higgins ... what happened, Mr Perry?'

Perry said, 'He got control. There was one hell of a fight between the fo'c'sle crowd, sir—'

'Injuries?'

'Quite a few sore heads. A lot of blood. Causton's gone. Higgins stove his head in with a belaying-pin. As deliberate an act of murder as I ever saw, sir.'

Halfhyde lay very still. Causton had proved, in the short time they had sailed together, to be a good man. Captain Good had said you could always trust the bosun, applying this to all bosuns. They formed a fine breed of men. Higgins was going to pay for that murder if Halfhyde had to repay kind with kind himself. Meanwhile there was a lot of thinking to be done. He sat up again, then fell back helplessly.

The girl said, 'Take it easy. You'll be better sooner. It takes time.'

Halfhyde made a supreme effort. 'I'm still the master,' he said. 'It's up to me.' He struggled again to a sitting position and swung his feet to the cabin deck. Nausea hit him again; he fought back.

Perry gestured to the steward. 'Whisky,' he said. Butcher brought a small one, neat.

Halfhyde took it and felt a shade steadier as the liquid went down his throat. He asked, 'What's the state of the ship now?'

'Same as before,' Perry said. 'You're still to be the figure-head. Higgins told me that. You're still needed. But if there's any more trouble, there'll be more killings.'

'And the crew?'

'Cowed as kittens, sir. Those that's loyal. The rest are watchful that they stay docile. There'll be no help there. Likely to go with the crowd now, some of them are.'

Halfhyde put his head in his hands. More killings . . . all too easy. Men could always be lost overboard at sea in bad weather; and cowed hands, or paid and compromised ones, wouldn't talk afterwards. At sea, there was nothing so dumb as a fo'c'sle crowd that had ganged up against the afterguard and any other authority. Higgins would know that well enough.

'The watches, Mr Perry. Higgins' men, or mine?'

The First Mate shrugged. 'A mixture. But I reckon Higgins will see to it that his lot take the bridge and engine-room rotas.'

'Baird?'

Perry said, 'The Chief's in a filthy mood, sir. He's against Higgins right enough, but like you he's needed. He's being watched below by one of his own firemen.'

'It's mutiny,' Halfhyde said through clenched teeth.

'You're right, it is.'

'Higgins can't take the ship into Valparaiso in a state of mutiny!'

Perry said warningly, 'I'd not be too sure about that, sir. He holds a lot of cards.'

'We'll see about that.'

'Yes, sir. But it might suit our book better to hang on till we have him in home waters. It's always better to deal with a law you know rather than one you don't.'

Halfhyde said savagely, 'Mutiny's mutiny in any man's law, and so is murder. Where's Higgins now, and Gaboon?'

'Higgins is on the bridge, sir. Foster's on watch. The man at the wheel is Fosdyke, one of Higgins' crowd. Gaboon's up there as well, somewhat the worse for wear. Both he and Higgins are armed and making no attempt to conceal their guns.' Perry paused. 'It's no use hoping Gaboon'll turn against Higgins after the beating he took. Gaboon depends on Higgins and he'll stand by him and take what he has to take. That's my view. You can see it in his eyes.'

Halfhyde nodded, an action that sent waves of pain shooting through his head. 'All right, Mr Perry. Do your best with the ship – I shall be on the bridge shortly. The ship's still mine, remember, and will be recovered. Keep that in your mind. There will be difficulties, but they will be overcome.'

'Yes, sir.' Perry left the cabin, Halfhyde heard his footsteps on the ladder leading down to the fore well-deck. Perry . . . there had been a kind of defeat in him when he had spoken of accepting matters until they were the right side of the Fastnet. Perry didn't want more deaths; nor did Halfhyde if they could be avoided. He told himself that a master's first concern should be for his crew. But now he had more than half his crew against him. Even so, he had a responsibility for those who had remained loyal. Perhaps Perry was right. Perhaps! But Halfhyde knew it was not within himself to accept even temporary defeat at anyone's hands, let alone those of a scoundrel like Higgins.

He looked up at Victoria. She asked, 'Feeling better?'

'Yes. You know Higgins better than I do. Do you think he'll be able to bluff his way through at Valparaiso?'

'Yes,' she said. 'I do.'

'With Perry and Foster and myself . . . and a few others including Baird to come out with the facts? How does he get away with that? If I'm not on the bridge, a very large rat is going to be smelled.'

She said restlessly, 'Oh, he'll cope. You can bet on that, Captain. It's obvious how – isn't it?'

He nodded. 'You.'

'That's right, me.'

Halfhyde's expression was grim. It had been standing out for a long while, in fact: the girl would be the hostage, the one who would get hurt. Higgins would know, or would be able to guess, Halfhyde's weak spot; and he had deliberately thrown the two of them together. All the same, Halfhyde couldn't see him getting away with it. The very atmosphere in the ship would tell the pilot, for one, that something was wrong. The sight of Gaboon alone would be enough to arouse suspicions – but perhaps Gaboon would be out of sight. Gaboon might well be on the starting platform, holding his gun in Baird's ribs just in case the Chief Engineer should make trouble by suddenly putting his engine astern or something similar that would throw the bridge into enough confusion to alarm any pilot or port official. Higgins would certainly anticipate that. Nevertheless Halfhyde saw Valparaiso as the only possible salvation.

* * *

Porteous Higgins had come up the hard way. He hadn't always been fat and flabby; he had been a slim youth when, back in 1867, he'd been one of the Fenian Men who had carried out the raid on Chester Castle. That had been a grand business; in his father's eyes he had grown up after that. His father, Hannibal Higgins, had been one of the so-called 'rebels of '48', a number of Irish exiles who had assembled in Paris to plan a rising in Munster against the English. After that, when the 'Phoenix Conspiracy', as the Munster rising was known, had failed, Higgins senior had crossed the Atlantic to America and become one of the founders of the Fenian movement whose objective was to establish an independent Republic of Ireland; the Fenians had found many followers among those who had left Ireland after the failure of the potato crop and the resulting famine that had killed so many of those who had stayed in their own land. Feelings were very bitter against the English absentee landlords who had done nothing for their tenants. The Fenians had had grandiose schemes, and their numbers had swelled after the American Civil War, which had cast adrift large numbers of Irishmen with a fighting spirit that longed for further adventure: even an invasion of Canada was planned and to a small extent carried out. When the conspirators – as the English had regarded them – had made their way back into Ireland, the young Porteous had arrived in the world. Hannibal lost no opportunity of indoctrinating him in the cause of Ireland and the concept of Ourselves Alone, or Sinn Fein. Porteous Higgins listened to his father's yarns of how he had suborned the British soldiers serving at the Curragh and other British military stations in Ireland; he read the press, that section of it that the English called treasonable, read the preachings of a desirable

63

war against the Saxon. But the movement failed to spread far, for the Catholic priesthood had set its face against violence and as a result the peasantry, the great mass of the Irish people, held aloof from it.

When Porteous Higgins was twenty he had been active in forming, with his father, new and more vigorous Fenian societies: the two main factions were the Clan-na-Gael and the United Irish Brotherhood, both directed from America. In the name of the former, Porteous Higgins had dedicated himself to the killing of the English, in ambushes and in straight fights, and he had become an expert gunman and saboteur. He had grown more vicious, more expert as the years went by; at the age of thirty he had gone to Australia to drum up support from the Irish emigrants in the southland. Emigrants and the descendants of the transported convicts of earlier times were the raw material of Porteous Higgins; and soon he had turned a large part of his attention to building up a personal fortune and personal power. He had succeeded well; he had holds over very many people both high and low, and he was known to stop at nothing. Murder came easy. So did cynically broken promises, corruption, extortion. There was no stopping Porteous Higgins, but he never made the mistake of appearing to grow too big. He could have bought himself the greatest house in Sydney, could have established himself in a very big way of trade with an imposing office building; but he preferred the Cross and the nondescript cover of the jeweller's shop in Porch Street. The bigger and more grandiose the web, the more envious and numerous would become the natural enemies of the spider. Size made a bigger target.

Porteous Higgins paced the bridge of the *Taronga Park* like any master. He believed he looked the part, believed he could possibly get away with acting it in front of the Valparaiso port authorities – up to a point, the point of appearance and authoritativeness alone. He would be caught out by a pilot; even though he could handle the business side of agents, documentation and general port requirements, he could pretend to no knowledge of ship handling. It would be too risky; he wouldn't take chances. There were other ways. His plans were already laid; and success had to be achieved. It would be. It was largely a personal matter. Two months earlier a letter had come for Porteous Higgins from Galway City in the province of Connaught: because of a lack of arms his father had been taken by the British Army in an attempted ambush on the road leading north from Galway to Oughterard. Hannibal Higgins, by this time an old man though active still for Ireland, had been tried and hanged in Dublin. Vengeance was going to be taken.

Higgins halted in his pacing, gazed for'ard, pulled at his lower lip. Valparaiso . . . still a little more than a week to go. There was time for thought. Valparaiso was a big port, usually filled with shipping. Since the recent fracas caused by Gaboon's activities things had changed a little aboard the *Taronga Park*. Like Halfhyde, Higgins was able to sense the ship's atmosphere: it was a brittle one and matters could go awry if his luck happened to be out. Someone, one of the men still loyal to Halfhyde, could risk the guns and make trouble. It was a pity about the bosun, Causton. Higgins had gathered that Causton had been a popular bosun, something few bosuns ever were. His death might have cemented some loyalties . . . Higgins as an Irishman knew all about martyrs.

He went below to the small chartroom alongside the Captain's cabin. He ferreted around in the folio beneath the table and found the chart, the next one that would be used, for the Chilean coast, the one showing the broad approaches from across the Pacific. This he studied, frowning, running a finger down southerly from Valparaiso. Then he went back to the bridge and blew down the voice-pipe to the engine-room, to be answered by Mr Baird.

'Yes?'

'This is the bridge. Is that the Chief Engineer?'

'Aye, it is. Would that be Higgins?'

'Yes. I—'

Higgins stepped back angrily: the slam of the voice-pipe cover in the engine-room had been loud. Higgins compressed his lips. Viciously he slammed a fist on to the voice-pipe, then he went down to Halfhyde's cabin. He went in. It was empty; a moment later Halfhyde entered from the master's deck.

'What do you want?' he demanded.

'The state of your bunkers, Captain.'

'Satisfactory.'

'More than enough to get the ship into Valparaiso?'

Halfhyde said, 'Any prudent shipmaster has a reserve in hand. You should know that.'

Higgins gave a thin smile. 'Precisely.' He pushed past Halfhyde and left the cabin. Halfhyde stared after him, feeling an apprehension of some further danger. What was Higgins after now? Some other port than Valparaiso? If so, why? All ports held dangers for a pirate, which was what Higgins was. He clenched his fists in frustration – impotence, aboard his own ship! There was nothing he could do without endangering men in a probably useless attempt to seize back control. The time hadn't yet come; and he had been banking on Valparaiso.

A few moments later he realized that the ship was already altering course. The horizon was swinging . . . he looked aft. There was a curve in the wake as it cut its white swathe through the deep blue. An alteration south-easterly. So Higgins did mean to head further down the coast of Chile. There were bunkering facilities at both Puerto Montt and Valdivia and both could probably be reached on Halfhyde's coal reserve. All the same, Higgins was taking something of a risk. To run out of bunkers and lie helpless would be of use to no-one, least of all Higgins himself. If a passing ship spotted their plight and put a party aboard, Higgins could come nicely unstuck. But that was too much to hope for.

Within the next half-hour Halfhyde was given orders to lay off a proper course for Puerto Montt. He had no option; and in the meantime Porteous Higgins had established from his confederates among the black gang that the reserve bunkers would be sufficient for the new destination, which was a little under six hundred miles south of Valparaiso. With the ship already on a fresh course the distance from their present position would be cut in any case: one side of a triangle instead of two.

* * *

The days passed; by now Gaboon's face was looking a healthier object behind the mat of hair and he and Higgins were back to taking watch and watch over the ship and her crew. There was no interference with Halfhyde apart from the fact that neither he nor Perry was allowed near the cargo hatches or the tween-decks. The ship steamed peacefully on her passage but the mood didn't improve.

All Halfhyde could do was to twiddle his thumbs and wait.

He saw a good deal of the girl. They had struck up a genuine companionship, easy with one another, the shared Yorkshire heritage giving them much in common. Halfhyde became accustomed to leaning with her over the rail of the master's deck as the ship steamed on through night after sultry night, beneath the great canopy of stars and a moon that silvered the sea with romantic light. He spoke of Wensleydale, of the shifting light over the fells, of the tinkling water running down the ghylls to feed, eventually, the River Ure; of the great waterfall at Hardraw, the triple falls at Aysgarth, the weird pits of the Buttertubs opposite Lovely Seat, a part well known years ago to the girl.

She talked about her family, her mother and brothers, even once or twice about her father. Whatever he had done, he was still her father, and once they had been close and she had loved him. She wanted now, above all else, to try to find her mother and brothers. It was so long since she had stowed away out of Liverpool . . . but she might yet pick up the traces.

Halfhyde said, 'You wanted to come back with me to Australia.'

'Well, it was a thought. I don't know. Australia didn't do a lot for me. Give me a little time in Britain, right?'

'I've a living to make,' he pointed out. 'But it may take time to sort out matters in regard to Higgins. Afterwards, I mean. The courts are slow . . . I shall have to remain in the UK till it's all over.'

'That'll cost you.'

He said, 'Yes. Or Uncle Henry, if he's willing.'

'Your wife's uncle, you said?'

'Yes.'

67

'Tell me about your wife, eh?'

He took a deep breath: except to himself, and perhaps that was bad enough, disloyalty was not in his nature. He had never spoken ill of Mildred to another party – not even to Uncle Henry in his dourest moods. Henry Willard had seen it, and said it all, for himself. Halfhyde said simply, 'She's my wife. I can't say more than that.'

'I like that about you,' she said. 'I get the idea you're not happy, though . . . and don't worry, I won't say any more.'

There was so much of which he would have liked to unburden himself had there not been that question of disloyalty. They stayed by the rail in a silent communion, listening to the engine sounds and the wash of water, and the tread of Gaboon overhead. The minutes drifted away; the girl's hair, blown by a wind that was no more than light airs that scarcely ruffled the dark water, brushed Halfhyde's chin. He took her in his arms and held her close. He was filled with misgivings for her safety; there was no feeling in Higgins, he would hold back from nothing, show no chivalry towards a woman.

SEVEN

Now the coast of Chile loomed: great mountain ranges stood behind the rocky land that fell away to the sea. Puerto Montt . . . Halfhyde picked up the landmarks for the second time in his seagoing career. The last occasion had been on the Queen's service, and Halfhyde's final departure from the port had left the Chilean authorities in some disarray, as indeed had his much more recent departure from the northern port of Arica when serving under Captain McRafferty in the *Aysgarth Falls*, but this time he had no particular fears of being sought by the Chileans. His good friend William Sturt of the Australian Joint Stock Bank had many useful contacts overseas and some of these were in Santiago. Halfhyde would be able to enter any Chilean port henceforward without casting glances over his shoulder for government agents.

Higgins, as the ship came up towards the entry to Reloncavi Bay, heaved his gross body up the ladder to the bridge and spoke to Gaboon. 'Engine-room,' he said briefly, and Gaboon went below. Higgins turned to Halfhyde. 'Don't make any trouble. You know what will happen if you do.'

Halfhyde gave no answer. Victoria Penn was being held in the First Mate's cabin with one of Higgins' men standing guard over her. When the pilot boarded a knife would be held against her throat and there would be no hesitation in using it should Halfhyde look like being indiscreet. He was hamstrung; but as the ship neared the entry and the long passage through to Puerto Montt he had other matters to occupy his attention. The land-locked waters were not easy even with the assistance of a pilot; the smallest error of ship handling and she would go hard aground on the many shoals that dotted the water. Halfhyde had toyed with the idea of disregarding the pilot's advice and deliberately putting her in hazard; but he had seen no real advantage in that. The Chileans were unpredictable and no doubt Porteous Higgins as well as William Sturt would have his contacts in the country; he would get away with it and have his cargo off-loaded into lighters and then carried onward, probably, in a Chilean ship – with Halfhyde left with a command broken upon the rocks.

He brought up his glasses as a small boat was seen coming outwards from the entry.

'The pilot?' Higgins asked.

'Yes.'

'Keep the girl in mind.'

* * *

Below in the engine-room, Baird heard the rattle as the anchor-cable ran out. Moving beneath Hornopiren, passing Calbuco Island to move along by Puluqui into Reloncavi Bay, the ship had proceeded through to the anchorage off Puerto Montt. A few moments later the telegraph rang from the bridge and the pointer moved to Finished with Engines. Baird nodded at his Second Engineer and then caught the eye of Gaboon, who was covering him with a revolver.

'All right, ye dumb loon,' Baird said savagely. 'Now we're here, I'll thank ye to remove yourself.' He gave Gaboon a push and the ape-like man, caught off balance, tripped over his own feet and fell from the starting platform, landing in a heap on the greasy steel deck plates. Making grunting noises of rage, he heaved himself up. He aimed his revolver at the Chief Engineer and squeezed the trigger. Baird took the bullet in his head and collapsed in a spreading pool of blood that drooled over the edge of the starting platform. Gaboon moved quickly to cover the Second Engineer, his mouth open and the root of his tongue swelling and retreating in an automatic effort at speech.

* * *

'A revolver shot?' the Chilean pilot asked. He raised an eyebrow at Halfhyde. Porteous Higgins gave a cough, one with obvious meaning.

Halfhyde said, 'I think not.'

The pilot shrugged, losing interest. Guns were not infrequently heard in Chile and what happened aboard a foreign ship was not his affair. 'I leave you now, Captain. I wish you a pleasant stay.'

'Thank you for your services,' Halfhyde said. He looked towards the port: a boat was coming off, belching a thick cloud of smoke from a dirty black funnel. A few minutes later the boat was alongside and a number of white-suited port officials were coming aboard by means of a jacob's ladder slung over by a couple of seamen. Accompanied by Porteous Higgins, Halfhyde went below to his cabin to deal with the Chilean authorities. Greetings were exchanged, the formalities dealt with and the ship's requirements for bunkers and steward's stores passed. All requirements would be met but there would be a delay in bunkering. It was unfortunate, but there was currently a shortage of bunker coal; replenishments were expected within three or four days. Colliers were due from Britain – from Barry dock in South Wales, with Rhondda coal. Higgins was restless at the delay, but had to accept it. He complained that Chile herself produced coal and that there should be plenty available. A small, dark Chilean shrugged and agreed that this was so, but it was not used for shipping, the steamship owners always preferred Welsh coal to any other. There was none like it for the furnaces.

This being settled, all the officials re-embarked in their steamboat and went back ashore. There had been no trouble over the *Taronga Park*'s cargo manifest; no examination had been made of the supposed cased machine parts and Halfhyde had expected none. He gritted his teeth against what he considered his own lack of backbone. A word to those port officials and he would at least have dropped a spanner in the works even if Porteous Higgins had subsequently been able to bribe his way out of it. But until he was in a stronger position the girl must be his first consideration.

Higgins was studying his face. 'You are a fool, Halfhyde,' he said. 'Your life would be easier if you came in with me – not just for now. I would pay well for future cargoes.'

'I want none of your money.'

Higgins laughed. 'You are your own worst enemy.'

Halfhyde turned on his heel and walked away. Higgins had the skin of a rhinoceros. There was no point in discussion, in argument. Glancing down into the after well-deck, Halfhyde saw the Second Engineer emerge from a doorway, looking sick. He called to him.

'Mr Young, that revolver shot. It seemed to come from the engine-room.'

'Yes, Captain. Gaboon . . . the Chief's dead.'

As Young spoke, Porteous Higgins approached again from the fore part of the master's deck. He said nothing, but his face was formidable. Later that morning, Gaboon received another beating. The animal sounds of pain revolted Halfhyde but he felt no sympathy. There were two of his crew to be avenged: Causton and now Baird.

* * *

The land-locked heat of the day cooled into evening; soon darkness came down and lights were seen flickering from the shore. In his cabin Halfhyde talked with Perry, who was now occupying the Chief Engineer's cabin aft: Victoria was still under guard in his own accommodation and would remain so, according to Higgins, until the *Taronga Park* had cleared away again to sea for the west-east passage of Cape Horn.

Halfhyde said, 'Those colliers that are expected, Mr Perry. Sail or steam – we don't know.'

'You're thinking their masters might assist, sir?'

'I know they would, if we could get a message to them. But Higgins will be watching for that.'

Perry nodded. 'He'll see to it there's no contact.'

'There may be a way. I can't see it at this moment, but something may come to me. Just a message, perhaps, to be sent by telegraph from Puerto Montt to our Embassy in Santiago and then reported to London, so that we're met off the Fastnet by a Naval escort – that would do the trick!'

'It would, but I see no prospect of getting a message across to them, sir.' Perry rubbed at his jaw thoughtfully. 'Except maybe by shouting for physical assistance and then—'

'I'll still not risk the girl, Mr Perry.'

'I understand that, sir,' the First Mate said, looking a shade uncomfortable, 'but there's others to be thought of as well, and if we have more murders—'

'You have my decision, Mr Perry. There's no more to be said. I shall find a more clandestine method than bawling across for all to hear.' Halfhyde got to his feet and moved over to the port, where he stood for a while looking out at the still, silent water and the distant line of shore lights. Turning away again, he asked with a grin, 'Are you willing to be lost overboard, Mr Perry?'

The First Mate was astonished at the question. 'Are your serious, sir?'

'Perfectly – but you'll not in fact drown. It's occurred to me that if one of the colliers is a steam vessel, she could reach home waters before us.'

'Perhaps, assuming she's not going farther north to discharge more cargo, and—'

'None of them are,' Halfhyde interrupted. 'I was told all the cargoes are for Puerto Montt. I dare say you know the port's used by the Chilean Navy, also by the steamers of the Pacific Steam Navigation Company.' Halfhyde paused. 'What do you know of the Second Engineer?'

'Young? He's a good man, sir. Knows his job, I'm told.'

'But the man himself? Will he remain loyal to the ship, and not be suborned by Higgins?'

'I believe so, yes. He was a long while with Captain Good. The *Taronga Park*'s his home. No wife, nowhere else to live. I reckon he'll stay with us, sir.'

Halfhyde nodded. 'In that case, it's possible some damage to the engines might be arranged, enough to give a steam collier a flying start – with you aboard, Perry.'

Perry frowned. 'There's a snag in that, surely? If Higgins knows I'm aboard—'

'Ah, but he won't! That is, he'll not be sure. We can pull enough wool over his eyes, I fancy.' Halfhyde went back again to the port; outside, the master's deck was deserted. Gaboon was still nursing the injuries received in his second beating. Porteous Higgins, Halfhyde saw, was on the fo'c'sle, turned towards the shore; a climbing moon showed the big, gross body, the pendulous stomach. Twice a murderer, if only by proxy: all Gaboon had done had been for Porteous Higgins, in basis. Halfhyde would dearly love to put a bullet in that gross stomach. Meanwhile, other ideas were forming. If Perry could be got off the ship he might in fact be of more use ashore than aboard one of the colliers. Halfhyde's first thought about making contact with the British Embassy in Santiago might well be – in fact would be – a much more direct way. Many things could happen at sea; the collier taking Perry to the United Kingdom could suffer a breakdown of her engine. If that should happen, the *Taronga Park* would steam into an unprepared position. But a message to the Embassy would certainly be acted upon immediately – though not too immediately, Halfhyde hoped. If his ship were to be arrested in Puerto Montt the proceedings would be long drawn, with a resultant financial loss to him as owner. Halfhyde's resources could not stand the drain; until he was well established as an owner, bankruptcy stood close at hand. Also, delay would result from instigating engine damage by the Second Engineer. The best course would be to take the *Taronga Park* out to sea and then rely upon Perry to set the wheels in motion, for the British Navy to be off the Fastnet on his arrival and catch Porteous Higgins red-handed off the Irish coast.

He put his thoughts to the First Mate. 'It should be a simple matter for you to slip over the side – not here in the bay, but while we're on our way out, in the shoals. The land's close in places as you've seen, and you can make your way back to Puerto Montt and find transport to the railway station at Osorno—'

'I'll never get away without being seen, Captain!'

Halfhyde smiled. 'I think you will, Mr Perry. I shall find a way of ensuring that the ship leaves the anchorage under cover of darkness. Your disappearance shouldn't be noticed until we're well out into the Pacific . . . I shall cover for you by taking your watch, and afterwards will write you off, simply if tragically, as lost overboard as the result of an accident. Well? Are you willing, in the interests of bringing a murderer to justice?'

Perry rubbed at his chin. 'I reckon I can scarcely refuse, but it's a bloody big risk that I'm seen and shot at.'

'I'll do my best to ensure you're not.' Halfhyde said. 'It's always possible to create a diversion at the appropriate time!'

* * *

Perry, Halfhyde thought, had seemed glad enough despite the obvious risk to be given the opportunity to get off the ship. Currently the *Taronga Park* was no-one's idea of joy. Threat lay like a blanket, smotheringly. The loyal men were closely watched by Higgins' traitors; and Gaboon, once again recovered and only a little subdued, was much in evidence as the ship continued next day to lie in the anchorage awaiting the arrival of her bunkers. The heat was as oppressive as the aura of fear that filled the ship. It was like a floating prison, a community totally isolated by a ring of guns.

There was still no contact with the girl. The guard on her cabin was changed at intervals; now and again Halfhyde, passing by the port, heard crying. Food was taken in, and brought out again mostly uneaten. Occasionally she was visited by Higgins, never for very long. On the evening of the third day after their arrival in Puerto Montt, Halfhyde encountered Higgins emerging from the cabin.

'How is she?' Halfhyde asked.

'Quite well. Let us hope she remains so, Captain.'

'When will she be released?'

Higgins shrugged. 'When I consider it expedient. That will probably be once we're well out at sea again.' He pushed past and went down the ladder to the after well-deck.

Halfhyde stared down at the retreating back, his eyes murderous. He had said to Perry that he would not risk the girl's life. What was he doing now? If anything should go wrong

75

with Perry's clandestine leaving of the ship . . . but nothing must go wrong. It could and would be brought off and he must do his duty. He felt sweat break out on his body, felt his hands clench involuntarily into fists. Thinking ahead to when the ship would be once again at sea brought him hard up against what had happened to Baird, whose body would be disposed of only after they had left Chile behind them. Currently the body was lying in the double bottom beneath the engine-room. The stench would soon seep upwards, and the men detailed to remove it and cast it overboard would have a diabolical task.

Halfhyde turned in for another night of tossing and turning, sleepless, in his bunk. Red-eyed and weary in the morning, he answered his steward's knock.

'Good morning, Butcher.'

'Morning, sir. Tea, sir.' Butcher sounded brisk. He handed a cup to Halfhyde. 'Collier, sir.'

'Where?'

'Just coming round the headland, sir. Steamer. Very dirty to look at, sir.'

'Colliers usually are.'

'Yessir. Let's 'ope this is the one for us.'

'Anxious to be at sea again, Butcher?'

'Anxious to get this bloody voyage over an' done with, sir.' Suddenly Butcher's face seemed to crumple. 'It's a proper bugger, sir, beggin' your pardon, never seen the like I 'aven't, not in forty years at sea, when the master ain't in command of 'is own ship.'

'I hope you never see it again,' Halfhyde said drily. 'I'm none too happy about it myself—'

'I know, sir. Spoke out o' turn, sir. Worse for you an' all – I know that. Wish I could help, sir.'

Halfhyde gave the steward a searching look. The man was much distressed – the first time he had shown it. Until now he had seemed to pretend that the situation didn't exist, that Halfhyde was still in charge, a brave and kindly attempt to save his Captain's face. Butcher was thoroughly trustworthy; it showed in his eyes, in every line of his face. One of the good hands, the old sort that were beginning to vanish from the seas

76

. . . Halfhyde said, 'Perhaps you can help, Butcher. Perhaps you can.' He paused. 'Where's Gaboon?'

Butcher jerked his head towards the port. 'Out on your deck, sir.'

'I fancied I heard him. We shall talk later, Butcher. For now, be as dumb as Gaboon.'

* * *

The collier let go her anchor off the starboard beam of the *Taronga Park*. Halfhyde and Perry watched the port officials leave her a little later, in their smoky steamboat. Towards noon a string of lighters was seen coming off behind a steam tug and heading out dead slow for the collier. Halfhyde, still pacing his deck with the First Mate, said, 'It'll be some time yet, Mr Perry. The Chileans don't hurry themselves.'

Perry nodded. 'Do you mean to sail as soon as we've got the coal aboard, sir?'

'Perhaps. It depends on the timing.' He lowered his voice; Gaboon was on the deck below, as watchful as ever. 'I think you know what I mean.'

Again Perry nodded: he'd taken it in. If coaling went on until dark – and if it started late enough he could make sure it did – then the Captain would have no need to trump up an excuse to offer Higgins for delaying their sailing – they could leave straight away, moving out through the night for the Pacific exit. With or without a pilot, as Halfhyde had already told him: Halfhyde was fully prepared to back his pilotage ability and take the ship out himself, and Porteous Higgins would be only too keen to avoid further delay.

For once, matters went Halfhyde's way. There was a long delay after the lighters had been made fast alongside the collier; the Chilean lightermen and stevedores sat or lay about their decks, some of them asleep, all of them suffering from inertia and no desire to hurry, while their foreman consulted lengthily with the collier's First Mate. It was the end of the afternoon siesta when the hatches were opened up aboard the collier, the derricks rigged, and the first bags of coal going down to the lighters. It took time to fill the lighters, time for them to cast off and move in leisurely fashion across to the *Taronga Park*. Perry went down to supervise, saw his derricks rigged and, with the Second Engineer, the chutes opened up to take the bags that would be emptied down them. Thereafter it was a job for all hands, the loyal men working alongside Higgins' gang; and by the time all the bunker coal was aboard and stowed, the sun was down, a flaming ball sinking over the invisible sea to the west.

Higgins, watching from the bridge, used the speaking-tube to Halfhyde's cabin. 'All aboard, I think,' he said.

'Yes.'

'Then we'll be away—'

'Not till Mr Perry's washed down my decks,' Halfhyde snapped, and banged back the speaking-tube plug. There was still too much light. He left his cabin and leaned over the after rail, calling down to the well-deck.

'Mr Perry?'

Perry looked up. 'Aye, sir?'

'Hose down, if you please. Make a thorough job of it.'

Perry acknowledged, keeping his face straight. He would make a very thorough job of it, removing every last trace of the coal-dust that lay thickly over the whole ship. Halfhyde went to the bridge, keeping an eagle eye on the work.

Higgins asked, 'What about the pilot? That'll mean more delay.'

'I can take her out,' Halfhyde said evenly.

Higgins mopped at his sweating face, which was dark with the coal-dust. 'The sooner the better.'

They spun it out; when Perry had finished, Halfhyde found fault and the hoses were turned on again, giving another swill-down to the deck and the deckhouses, the hatch covers, the lower masts. By the time Halfhyde was satisfied the sun was down and the darkness was thickening fast. 'All ready,' Halfhyde said to Higgins.

'Don't delay any longer, then!'

'As you say.' Halfhyde leaned from the rail. 'Mr Perry, stand by the anchor.'

'Aye, aye, sir.' Perry went for'ard and climbed to the fo'c'sle, calling for the carpenter to man the windlass. Halfhyde blew down the engine-room voice-pipe.

'I'm about to weigh anchor, Mr Young. Obey telegraph.' He waited to take Perry's report from the fo'c'sle and when this was received he passed the order to weigh. Link by link the cable was wound in on the windlass; as Perry reported the anchor up-and-down, Halfhyde moved to the telegraph and pulled the handle over to Slow Ahead.

The *Taronga Park* began to shake to the turning of the main shaft and the thrust of her single screw. The anchor broke surface and was left at the waterline in case of sudden need in restricted waters. The ship moved out, taking it slow. Halfhyde felt a surge of excitement, of apprehension, run through his body. The girl was still much in his mind; her life could depend on his and Perry's success. Perry had been briefed in his orders; and by now Butcher knew the part he had to play. From now on, it was in the hands of God. Halfhyde sent up a prayer that God would be found positively on the side of the righteous; often enough in the past he had found a degree of unselectivity on the Almighty's part, as though He had nodded off to sleep at some crucial moment. As his ship moved slowly outwards Halfhyde found himself thinking, incongruously enough, of Mildred. That had been a nodding-off moment if ever there was one. God should have known better, should have sent some sign of displeasure to Mildred, who was an inveterate churchgoer when not on horseback chasing a fox, or attending a point-to-point. Another bone of past marital contention: Halfhyde's church attendances had been irregular and reluctant, not on account of any antipathy towards God but because he disliked the unction of the clergy. Now he wished he had been more sedulous; prayer could sometimes come too late and appear more like a clumsy attempt to appease an admiral.

They moved on towards the narrows. Halfhyde stood behind the binnacle, conning his ship with close attention. Through the darkness he saw Perry with a lantern, making an extra check of the anchor gear, running an eye over the slips and stoppers and cable clenches that would be used to secure the anchors for sea, the efficient First Mate very much in evidence from the bridge. Soon Perry would move aft, carrying out more checks, invisible from the bridge on the starboard side. To port, Butcher would come out from the master's cabin, bearing a tray, and after waiting for the signal descend the ladder to the well-deck. Higgins would remain firmly on the bridge, that could be relied upon; and Gaboon would be equally firmly in the engine-room. Aside from the fo'c'sle party the only hands on deck would be the helmsman and the lookout in the crow's nest for'ard, both concentrating ahead. Or they should be the only ones; Halfhyde sent up a supplementary prayer that no-one would emerge from the fo'c'sle at the wrong moment.

The ship left the lee of Puluqui and began passing Calbuco. Ahead the great lofty bulk of Hornopiren reached into the sky. Soon they would come into the vicinity of the shoals; Halfhyde, who had made an exhaustive study of the chart and the Admiralty Sailing Directions during the days of waiting for the collier, knew precisely where and when to act to Perry's best advantage.

He felt a shake in his fingers, clasped his hands hard behind his back to conceal it – unnecessarily, since Higgins was staring for'ard over the bow. By now Perry was no longer in sight. He would be ready and waiting; he would not have far to drop into the shallows – the *Taronga Park*, already well down in the water with her heavy cargo, was now once again right down to her marks after taking full bunkers, and there was little freeboard.

Watching his cross-bearings, Halfhyde brought the ship into the shoal area. This was to be the tricky part, and not only from the viewpoint of split-second timing in getting Perry ashore unnoticed: as on entry, one false move could pile up the ship and she might become a total loss. Now the bearings were coming on, slowly, inexorably. The moment had to be one hundred per cent right: it was up to him alone.

He shouted, '*Wheel hard-a-port for your life!*'

The helmsman reacted fast, wrenching the wheel hard over.

Higgins turned in alarm. 'What the—'

'Shoal ahead,' Halfhyde said briefly. 'Midships!'

The ship, under port helm, had swung hard and fast to starboard. Before she had been checked by the wheel coming back in response to Halfhyde's last order, Butcher had gone into action. A wild yell came from the port side, followed by the sound of a body falling down a ladder to the accompaniment of the clattering of a metal tray and the shattering of crockery. Cursing, Higgins ran over to the port side of the bridge.

'There's a man in the water!' he shouted.

Halfhyde said, 'Throw him a lifebuoy, Higgins – fast!'

There were lifebuoys in the racks on either side of the bridge; by the time Higgins had pulled out the one on the port side, Halfhyde had passed the order to stop the engine. He wiped streaming sweat from his face and blew out a long breath. All the attention was now on the port side, where Butcher could be seen making a fine show of struggling in the water and trying to reach the lifebuoy on the end of its line.

Perry should have an unremarked swim to the shore, which was not far off. In the meantime Higgins was blaspheming like any fo'c'sle hand: Halfhyde's carelessness in misjudging his course, leading to a sudden alteration . . . the clumsiness of any man who allowed himself to be thrown overboard from a ladder . . . the risk to the ship and her cargo.

Elated at what seemed to be success, Halfhyde accepted it all meekly.

EIGHT

Butcher was hauled aboard, little the worse for his adventure; the *Taronga Park* proceeded safely outwards in Halfhyde's hands. Coming out from the narrows into the open sea, Halfhyde turned southerly for Cape Horn. There was a strong wind blowing: luck was with Halfhyde still. The *Taronga Park* pitched and rolled as she came away from the land, labouring hard in the long, high waves and a heavy swell sweeping in from the Pacific deeps. This was the sort of weather in which a man could understandably lose his footing on wet decks, and if he were unhandy be swept overboard, sliding helplessly beneath the guardrails. Perry was far from unhandy; but accidents could happen to the best of men, and as Baird had once remarked, Higgins was no seaman; he wouldn't think as such.

At midnight, the bridge watch was relieved. Higgins went below and Gaboon, released earlier from the engine-room, took his place. A new helmsman came up: one of the renegades. The Second Mate, Foster, relieved Halfhyde, who went down to his cabin. Foster already had his orders; waiting for them to be put into effect, Halfhyde once again found that sleep eluded him. He was wide awake when at a quarter to three that morning the alarm went up and he heard the shout on deck: '*Man overboard starboard!*'

As the engine-room telegraph rang out above his head, Halfhyde pulled on his oilskin and ran for the bridge. Close behind him came Porteous Higgins. 'What is it, Mr Foster?' Halfhyde shouted against the tearing wind.

'Someone went over to starboard, sir—'

'Do you know who it was?'

'No, sir. Shall I call away the lifeboat, sir?'

'In this sea? I think not, Mr Foster.' Halfhyde brought up his binoculars and searched the water to starboard. Aft, hands were tending the lines of lifebuoys cast out in the hope that the man, the invisible man, might be able to grab for them. There was no light in the sky as yet. 'The poor fellow will not have had a chance, he'll be well astern by this time. I'll not risk more men's lives by sending away a boat. But we'll turn and search nevertheless.'

Higgins, heavy and dough-faced by the starboard rail, objected. 'It's a waste of time, Halfhyde. I don't want this voyage to go on for ever.'

'A man's life is at stake,' Halfhyde said coldly, tongue in cheek, and passed the orders for turning his ship on to the reciprocal of her course. Inside him his heart sang: it had been beautifully acted out. It was Higgins who, a few moments later, asked where the First Mate was, why he was not on deck. More acting: Halfhyde and Foster registered surprise, shock, disbelief. It couldn't be Perry . . .

'Go below and call the roll of the men, Mr Foster,' Halfhyde ordered, stony-faced.

* * *

Many miles behind, from away back inside the narrows leading to Reloncavi Bay and Puerto Montt, Perry had reached the shore in safety. It had not been too difficult to remain submerged, with an occasional lifting of his head to take a breath, while the diversion caused by Butcher's clumsiness occupied the attention of those aboard the outward-bound steamer. After the ship had moved on, Perry had swum easily for the shore, quickly coming into water shallow enough for a man to stand and wade. Once ashore he had wrung the water from his clothes and after a brief rest had struck across country, difficult country for the most part, in as direct a line as possible for Puerto Montt, though, faced by high ground, he had found himself forced to take the much longer line around the shore for a good deal of the way. By the time the sun was up he had made little net progress after walking through the night. In the day's warmth he stripped and laid out his clothes to dry while he slept. Speed was not essential; the *Taronga Park* had a long voyage ahead of her to the Fastnet and her Irish landfall. Once he reached Puerto Montt, he would find transport to the railway at Osorno; and once he had made his report to the British Embassy in Santiago, the telegraph lines across the oceans would be busy.

Waking refreshed, Perry got on the move again. By the next nightfall he was walking into Puerto Montt, tired, hungry and thirsty, his water-bottle empty, the bread wrapped in oiled silk all gone. There were few people about; the occasional man stared curiously at him: he was obviously British, obviously a seaman, probably from the collier, which was still in the port.

He must find food and bed for the night.

* * *

The girl had been released now. Higgins, totally unsuspicious about Perry, felt safe. Perry had gone overboard in heavy weather and could not possibly have survived; they had been well out to sea, no danger of a body drifting landwards and raising queries. When the First Mate's supposed end had been confirmed, Higgins felt safe also in authorizing the disposal of the Chief Engineer's body over the side. He believed there would be no more difficulties now, not even when the *Taronga Park* entered British waters. His confidence was almost unnerving. Once again the girl would be the hostage, the lever that would ensure compliance on Halfhyde's part. Things were in Higgins' favour: even the drowning of the First Mate had been propitious, leaving Halfhyde without his principal aide.

Higgins grew expansive as the ship made progress down towards Cape Horn. The arms and ammunition he carried would quickly be in use against the British government forces in Ireland – at the Curragh, the other military camps, the naval base at Haulbowline, against the Royal Irish Constabulary, even the seat of government in Dublin Castle.

'A blow for freedom, Captain Halfhyde,' he said.

'A blatant act of rebellion.'

'Not of rebellion. An act of self-defence against a power that has no right to be in Ireland. Ireland is for the Irish. The British landowners will be killed, thrown out, dispossessed. The land will return to the Irish people.'

'And you? You'll lead them?'

Higgins shrugged. 'They have their own leaders. No, I'm not ambitious in that direction. I am the supplier – a role not to be despised.'

'You mean you don't risk your own neck in fighting?'

Higgins was not in the least put out. 'Why should I? I'm of more use doing what I know. The cobbler should stick to his last. Fighting isn't the only way to help Ireland.' He returned to his earlier theme. 'You're a seaman, that is where your use lies. You could be of use to me and need never concern yourself with the final destination of your cargoes, Captain. And you would never lack a cargo. Isn't that important to you – you who make your living from the sea and ships?'

'You're a remarkably poor judge of character, Higgins.'

'Each man has his price,' Higgins responded calmly. 'What's yours?'

'My honour has no price, nor has my loyalty to the Queen.'

Higgins gave a loud laugh. 'I think you are unctuous, Captain. You have a governessy sound. A master mariner is usually a man of the world—'

'Not of your world, Higgins. I shall have none of it.'

Higgins nodded, gave Halfhyde a shrewd look. For a while he was silent, rolling easily to the ship's motion, his big body bulking against the rail, thick neck overhanging his collar in bulges of fat. Then he said in a quiet voice filled with menace, 'No doubt it has occurred to you to wonder what is to happen to you after our landfall?'

'A fair question,' Halfhyde said.

'Yes. I think I need not put it into words. Ponder it, Captain. It's usually better to take the safer path.'

Halfhyde said nothing. It had been obvious all along that he couldn't, for Higgins' safety, be allowed to go free once the ship had berthed. Murder was easy enough in Ireland, as easy as at sea. The army and police had for many years fought a sordid battle against the so-called loyalist killers. But was he, with that knowledge clear in his mind, really expected by Higgins calmly to assist the ship to berth in an Irish port? Any man already condemned to death would fight back before doing that, accepting an earlier death if by so doing he could in some way upset the plans. But the answer was, of course, as plain as it had been all along: Victoria Penn, the one who would suffer first, the one who could be used against Halfhyde even when – or if – the British fleet made its appearance off the Fastnet.

On the change of watch Gaboon came up to take over from Porteous Higgins. Foster arrived to relieve Halfhyde, who went below to his cabin. He had half expected to find Victoria there, but the cabin was empty. Empty and bare – and lonely. He would have welcomed company. The departure of Perry had deprived him of company, one of the few aboard whom he could trust. Foster could be trusted, but inevitably there could be no companionship between men who stood watch-and-watch – and Foster was of a different stamp from Perry. Younger, without the deeper understanding that went with many years at sea. The sea was a brotherhood and the longer a man had been part of it the greater the contentment that went with the company of a fellow seafarer. Perry was a sad if necessary loss, one strong arm the less if it came to a fight in the end. Halfhyde could now count his known allies almost on the fingers of one hand: Foster, Young, Butcher, Thompson the ship's carpenter and two of the fo'c'sle seamen, gnarled old men who had been sailing the seas as far back as memory took them, shellbacks from the square-rigged sailing ships, seamen to the last drop of their blood who had no time for landlubbers and would never bow to a man like Porteous Higgins, still less Gaboon.

Halfhyde turned in, and, dead tired, slept until it was time to return to the bridge.

* * *

Perry came upon an old woman sitting in the doorway of a hovel behind the waterfront, an old crone wizened and toothless, dressed overall in seedy black turning green with age and dirt. She appeared to grin at him, though this could have been no more than the chewing motion of her lips brought about by her toothless state. Perry, unused to day-long marches, being near exhaustion, stopped. He had a word or two of Spanish as a result of many past voyages to Chile, Peru and the Argentine. Haltingly he asked if by chance the old woman had a bed for the night. She looked doubtful, scared even at an approach from a seaman. She half turned, and called in a high voice into the room behind her, and a man emerged, a small man, rat-like and dark, much younger than the old woman. He turned out to be her son. There was, he said, a palliasse. Would that suffice?

'Yes,' Perry said thankfully. 'A meal also?'

'*Si*,' the man said. A price was agreed; Perry drew money from his pocket – copper, silver, gold. Australian currency, but the man's eyes lit up. A florin changed hands and Perry was admitted past the old crone. He was led by the son into a room at the back, a small square place that smelled of unwashed bodies and a lack of sanitation. Darkness had fallen now, and the man lit a tallow lamp that added its smoke to the stench that filled Perry's nostrils. He saw the palliasse, the straw sticking through the thin cover. Well, it was a bed of a sort and he must have rest. A meal, he was told, would be brought shortly. He sat on the palliasse and waited. After a long interval the man came in with a bowl of mushy beans and a hunk of foul-smelling bread together with a pitcher of water. Better than nothing; Perry ate and drank. Then, unable to keep awake any longer, he removed his coat and trousers, flopped back on to the straw and went sound asleep. He had no idea how long he had been sleeping when a small noise brought him, with his seaman's instinct for untoward sounds and emergencies, fully awake.

He could see nothing in the pitch darkness but he was convinced there was someone in the room. Close by him . . . where he had deposited his coat and trousers.

His money. He had been a fool to have brought out a handful of coins; sheer weariness had over-ridden caution, destroyed common sense.

He moved very fast, bringing himself to a crouching position and then jumping for the coat and trousers. He crashed into a body, heard a sharp cry, reached out to get his arms around the intruder. The body squirmed violently, threw Perry off. Reaching out again blindly, Perry got a grip on what he believed was an ankle. He heaved; there was another cry, the leg jerked but failed to free itself from Perry's grip. Then the body seemed to move round behind him and he felt the slash of a knife. He jerked sharply away, lashed out with a fist and contacted bone. At the same time he was aware of a commotion in the other room, the front room, of a loud shriek from the old crone and then the banging of a door, followed by shouts in the filthy alley beyond. He hung on to the leg, tried again to hit the man, but failed. Then the leg was pulled free by a sudden jerk. Perry fanced he saw movement, something darker than its surroundings coming towards him. He felt a movement of air as an arm struck out, and he made another wild grab and found he had got hold of a wrist. Feeling with his free hand he flinched as he drew his flesh painfully across steel. He twisted the wrist with all his strength, there was a low hiss of pain and he heard the knife fall to the floor.

Crouching, he contacted it.

He held it in front of his body, waiting for the next attack. As once again he sensed movement he tensed and lunged with the knife. He felt it penetrate and in the same moment he was taken very heavily on the shoulder and the side of his neck by something of immense weight and strength and he went out cold.

* * *

The weather worsened as the *Taronga Park*, dropping south, reached the tearing westerlies that would follow her around Cape Horn. Great crests reared, the dreaded greybeards of the Horn, their long tops flattened into driving spume that raced ahead of the plunging steamer. Those waves threatened every moment to overrun her decks, came down in solid water on the after hatches, rushing, pouring, seeking out every weak spot, every small access to the below-decks sections of the ship. It was a time of extreme discomfort and of total wetness for all hands. Halfhyde remained on the bridge throughout, nursing his ship through the never-ending gale, thankful enough that this time he wasn't making the passage under sail. As the *Taronga Park* fought round she raised a windjammer beating into the westerlies and being forced away as her master made an attempt to pick up some favourable shift of wind that would carry him round into the Pacific, his masts bare of all canvas except for the lower tops'ls which looked in danger of being ripped away at any moment.

Halfhyde watched in sympathy. The east–west passage was the real test of men and a seaman's skill, at any rate in the windjammers.

'A hell of a life, Mr Foster,' he said. 'But it has its compensations. It's real seafaring when all's said and done.'

'I was glad enough to leave it, sir.' Foster brought up his binoculars and studied the wallowing ship. Her waist could scarcely be seen for the swirling, racing seas pounding aboard; poop and fo'c'sle looked like islands joined together by some invisible bond. No fires, no food, no hot drink – and she might be trying to batter round for days yet, even weeks. Cape Horn itself was barely visible through the spume and the overcast; just a blur behind the terrible wetness, the last grey piece of South America, the end of the world, reaching down from below Hoste Island and the dreadful inlets to the north.

At last they were round and altering course a little to the east-north-east to come up past Staten Island and make into the South Atlantic. There would be more bad weather yet, though it would moderate a little once they had moved north of the Falklands. More days of wet discomfort. With Cape Horn behind him, Halfhyde ordered a full check on the holds and bilges. He cared nothing about Higgins' guns and ammunition but could not allow water to gather below and affect his trim and seaworthiness. The pumps had been working all the way round the cape and had disgorged some seepage; but the report from the carpenter indicated that there was nothing that couldn't be dealt with.

Once past Staten Island and with the ship riding more easily, Halfhyde left the bridge to Foster, ate a cold meal brought up from the galley by his steward and dropped into his bunk for a spell. Sleep this time brought nightmares, restless mental disturbances in which every man's hand was against him, vivid scenes of determined hunters with himself the quarry, turning upon his pursuers like a tiger but with no effect. The image shifted: he was in a battle, a land battle with British soldiers being mown down by the guns of Porteous Higgins, their corpses sinking into an Irish bog . . . Waking in a muck-sweat he fought through the terrible visions to a realization that Higgins was not going to succeed. Perry would by this time have reached Santiago. Once off the Fastnet, retribution would come with the advent of, probably, a customs cutter, backed by the might of the British fleet.

And that had to be planned for. When the ships were sighted and Higgins took in their purpose – that would be the time of danger. Halfhyde's dispositions must be made; they must all be ready. At least, he had something constructive to do.

NINE

It was far from easy: there was too much watchfulness on the part of Higgins and Gaboon and the majority of the ship's crew. Butcher was Halfhyde's go-between; he was able to liaise with the two loyal seamen: O'Dowd and Byers, plus the carpenter, Thompson. O'Dowd was an Irishman, but had no time for the rebel faction: he was loyal to the crown. He had a grandson serving with a battalion of the Connaught Rangers, in camp at the Curragh, and he would never have any truck with those who ran guns to men who might fire upon his own flesh and blood. Halfhyde himself could pass written messages to the Second Mate at the change of watches, a little sleight-of-hand unnoticed by Higgins or Gaboon. The girl, still accommodated aft, could make occasional contact with the Second Engineer. Broadly, Halfhyde's plan was to have his loyal men positioned, as the approach to the Fastnet was made, in such a way that they could seize control at the moment that the sighting of the British ships threw Higgins off balance. In particular, Victoria was to be protected and every effort made to ensure that Higgins was inhibited from using her as a hostage as he had done in Puerto Montt.

'I don't know why you worry about me,' Victoria said one evening as the *Taronga Park*, now in fair weather, moved north towards the tropics. They were in Halfhyde's cabin and were as usual keeping their voices low. 'I'm nothing. You know that. God knows what sort of future I face.'

'Never despair, Victoria. You don't know what's round the next corner.'

91

She sneered. 'Bloody platitudes.'

'But nevertheless true. And I'm not going to see you used.'

'Don't muck up anything just because of me,' she said. 'Those guns are more important – to you and a lot of other people over there in Ireland. If you're too occupied with me, you'll go and lose the whole show.'

He shook his head. 'No. The Navy'll see to that. It's all over for Higgins and Gaboon, whatever happens to all of us.'

She blew out a long breath, moved restlessly in her chair. 'Aren't you being too sure? What if something goes wrong – say if Mr Perry doesn't get to Santiago?'

'Perry can look after himself,' he said with assurance. 'If he doesn't get there physically, it's not beyond his wit to send a message to the Embassy.'

'You still can't be absolutely certain.'

He said firmly, 'Don't look on the black side. We're going to win. I'm damned if I'm going to be beaten by Porteous Higgins, Victoria. We're going to steam right into the arms of the Channel Squadron . . . battleships and cruisers, with heavy guns. It should be a fine sight.'

She looked at him, biting her lip and frowning. 'You're a weird one,' she said. 'Why ever did you leave the Navy, eh?'

He laughed. 'Senior officers and I did not agree, and I was too quick to say so on many occasions. I can't abide pig-headed men, however many gold stripes they carry on their sleeves.'

'Are admirals pig-headed?' she asked curiously. 'I've never met an admiral, I reckon . . .'

He smiled at her naïvety. He said, 'Some are worse than pig-headed. Not all by any means, but some. They can be downright dangerous! Admirals who order the watertight doors in their squadrons to be burnished, thus destroying their watertight capacity. Admirals who burnish not only the watertight doors but also the anchor cables . . . admirals who refuse to hold gunnery practice so as to avoid damage to the paintwork, on the principle that smart ships lead to quicker promotion than ships whose guns' crew can hit a target. There are far too many like that, Victoria.'

She grinned at him. 'We'd better hope the admiral in the

Channel isn't one of that sort,' she said.

* * *

After many days and nights Perry had come to on another bed,
this time a hard one composed of planks set together and raised
some eight or nine inches from the floor. He felt desperately sick
and his right shoulder was painful; there was dried blood upon
his body and his mouth was as dry as dust. Light filtering
through from a grille set high up in one wall showed him that he
was in a cell. There were irons about his ankles, and the door,
big and heavy, was iron bound. Gradually the events of the
night – which night, how many nights ago? – came back to him.
The attack, and his own resistance.

Why was he, the injured party, in a cell?

Sickness overcame him; he retched violently, felt close to
death. The food, the water he'd been given in the hovel . . . he
tried to call out but could scarcely hear his own voice. He had to
get free; there was an important message. What was it? He felt
light-headed, utterly discomposed. He retched again and was
left shaking and drenched with sweat.

Lying limp, he stared up at the ceiling. Guns – of course. A
cargo of guns. And he had to get to Santiago. The matter was
vital, his Captain was depending on him. Ireland. Higgins.

He had to get away.

He called out again but no-one came. Despair settled on
Perry like a cloud. The sick feeling was terrible; he would never
get to Santiago but someone, surely, would see that a message
was sent?

At last he heard footsteps, the jangle of keys, heavy bolts
being drawn on the outside of the iron-bound door. The door
opened and two men came in, men in dirty, gaudy uniforms,
who stared down at him curiously. One of them, a heavily
moustached man, spoke to him.

'Inglees?'

'Yes.'

'Sailor?'

'Yes.'

'Not from collier. Check made of crew. Where?'

93

Through a haze of sickness in which the cell and the men appeared to revolve around him, Perry said, 'The steamer *Taronga Park* . . .'

'Yes? She leave many days ago. How is this?'

'I went overboard . . .' Perry's voice tailed away, his arm flopped to the floor. There was a low conversation in Spanish between the two men.

The one who had done the talking said, 'You are sick. A doctor will come. Then more questions.'

Perry tried to tell them he had a vital message, that he must leave and head north, but the words refused to come. Leaving him in sweat and vomit, the men went away, bolting the door behind them. Perry's mind drifted off into a jumble of images, of the ship and her cargo, of the old crone, of Higgins and Gaboon and the murdered bosun, of a knife sliding into flesh, of shoals and stormy seas.

* * *

Trouble came as the *Taronga Park* moved into the Doldrums. That enervating area of patchy wind and oily seas was the bane of the square-rig masters; steamship men had no particular need to curse the Doldrums but nevertheless it was a part of the world where heat and close stickiness led to frayed tempers, a time when brewing feuds came to boiling point. A time – on this voyage – when men found it impossible to hold their hands away from striking back.

In the case of the Second Engineer it was Gaboon who provoked it by his very presence in the engine-room during one hot forenoon watch. Gaboon had gone down simply to impress Young that he was still being watched and that he should mind his ways. He had approached the starting platform, thick and hairy and with the root of his tongue swelling and retreating with some unuttered speech and his gun in his hand. Something had snapped in Young's mind and he had gone berserk. The result reached the bridge when the Second Mate had the watch: the engine came to a sudden stop and the ship began to lose way through the water. When Foster called the engine-room via the voice-pipe he was given the facts by a greaser.

94

He blew down the speaking-tube to the master's cabin.

Halfhyde answered. 'Yes?' As he woke from sleep, his senses registered that the engine was silent. 'What's happened?'

'Mr Young, sir. Used a fire axe and smashed the place up.'

'Does Higgins know this?'

'Yes, sir—'

'I'm coming up,' Halfhyde said. He pulled on his trousers and went up the ladder fast. Higgins was at the engine-room voice-pipe, his face savage. He swung round on Halfhyde.

'You'll suffer for this,' he said furiously. 'How long will it take to make a repair?'

Halfhyde shrugged. 'I'm no engineer.'

'You'd better become one, then!'

'Easier said than done.' Halfhyde smiled icily. 'A repair may be impossible for all I know, in which case we shall have to wait until a passing ship offers us a tow. For now, all I can do is to have a look for myself.'

He turned on his heel and went down the ladder. In the engine-room he found matters potentially worse than he had realized. Gaboon was nursing a smashed hand, a hand almost severed at the wrist. His revolver had gone and blood was spurting while one of the engine-room hands wound a piece of torn-off shirt as a tourniquet. The Second Engineer was lying in a heap on the metal deck with his head split open. A big greaser approached Halfhyde, holding the fire axe threateningly.

Halfhyde stared at him. 'I assume you killed Mr Young.'

'Too right.'

'Very intelligent, to kill my only remaining engineer. If ever we make port, you'll swing for that. And if Higgins decides to take his own revenge first, I shall not interfere.' Halfhyde turned his back on the axe carrier, moving away to examine the damage. A number of hand-wheels, their connecting rods broken in what must have been an attack given the strength of madness, were badly distorted. Halfhyde was aware that the ship's resources were slender, and now there was no engineer to oversee the work. It would be hit and miss to a large extent. Most of the gauges had been smashed and there was a hiss of steam from a fractured pipe, steam that was luckily being

95

drawn out through the skylight, which stood open in the hot weather. Young had made plenty of use of his axe before he had been stopped in his tracks. All the connections to the dynamo had gone and the linkage to the main shaft looked like a junk yard.

Halfhyde took a deep breath and called the engine-room complement together in the now-silent engine space. 'I understand you're all Higgins' men down here. Am I right?'

There was no reply at first; the men had sheepish expressions, not meeting the Captain's eye. Then the big man with the axe spoke up. 'Aye,' he said. 'That's right. That's what we are. You'll just have to get used to it.'

Halfhyde nodded. 'Right. Now we know where we stand, I'll tell you this: you've done my ship no service by killing the engineer – but of course you didn't mean to do me any service. What now concerns you is that you've done Higgins no service either. It's up to you to make good the damage where possible, before Higgins sorts you out. Understand, Pearson?'

Pearson, the axeman, leader of the black gang, nodded. Halfhyde turned for the ladder and went back on deck, making for the bridge. Higgins was in the well-deck, coming aft. Halfhyde gave him a summary of the damage and he continued down into the engine-room to look for himself. On the bridge, Halfhyde found Foster on his own, and told him what he had told Higgins.

'No chance of moving, sir?' Foster asked.

'At present, none.'

'Might be better if they can't make a repair, sir. That'd muck up Higgins' plans for Ireland, wouldn't it?'

'Ours as well. No, that's not the way.'

'Wouldn't the Navy find us, sir?'

Halfhyde laughed. 'By sheer chance – yes, perhaps! A needle in a haystack – the South Atlantic is no pond, Mr Foster. Besides, if we can't move we can't eat – eventually. So move we must. But I have my doubts if we will.'

Soon afterwards Higgins came back, accompanied by Gaboon. Taking over the watch from Foster, Halfhyde did his best to disregard both Higgins and Gaboon. With nothing to do

96

now but keep a lookout for other shipping he tried to make some assessment of the likely action by the authorities in the United Kingdom when after Perry's message had reached Whitehall the *Taronga Park* failed to make her landfall off the Fastnet. Would a search be mounted in spite of that needle-in-a-haystack element? After all, the Navy had plenty of ships.

There was, perhaps, just a chance. A lot depended on the costiveness or otherwise of Their Lordships, as pompous a load of shore-bound admirals as the world had ever known ... Halfhyde reflected on the high-ranking officer who was still his father-in-law. Vice-Admiral Sir John Willard, now retired, had failed to make a Lord of the Admiralty during his service, but had he done so he would have dithered and procrastinated with the rest of them, thinking of further promotion and of how the Treasury disliked the service estimates at the best of times – and of how expensive it was to feed too many furnaces with coal in any quartering of the South Atlantic's immensity of water.

* * *

The doctor in Puerto Montt, a seedy, shifty-eyed man in a smelly black frock coat, had had no difficulty in reaching a diagnosis when confronted with Perry in his cell: dysentery, he said. The prognosis was poor, although the sufferer was basically a healthy man. He would shortly die; it was inevitable and to find a woman to nurse him would be a waste of time and resources. But Perry gave him the lie by recovering after a torment of delirium, diarrhoea, and griping, twisting pains in the large intestine. From time to time he had been conscious of people looking down at him, and the frock-coated one talking about the possibility of gangrene attacking the intestine. There was much excited chatter around his plank bed, and a waving of arms, and an insistence by the uniformed men that the Chief of Police would not wish a British subject, whatever his crime, to die whilst in Chilean custody; and the doctor was forced to do something about it. Treatment of a sort was given in time: castor oil and opium were administered, and after that copious doses of ipecacuanha powder, and then a succession of enemas consisting of corrosive sublimate, opium, calomel and bismuth;

97

and the intestines were douched with antiseptic solutions. In due time Perry was given arrowroot to eat and a little soda-water and brandy to drink.

He had no idea how much time had gone by when he began to feel better and was able to sit up. No-one would answer his requests for information nor listen to his pleas about the importance of his message. There would be, he was told again, more questions later.

The questioning came next day. Perry was being accused of murdering the old crone's son, who had died from the knife wound inflicted during the fight in the total darkness of the back room. The man's own knife, Perry said. Was that not proof that he had been attacked? And his money; the man had been after that and had been disturbed in the purloining of it.

But where was the proof? And why had he left his ship?

Perry said there was no connection between his leaving his ship and the fracas in the hovel. He had merely sought a bed for the night and the next day would have found transport to Osorno and the railway line to Santiago. His questioner seemed to think he was side-tracking the interrogation, and brought him back to the point: why had he killed the man in the back room? It went on and on, a repetition of question and answer impeded by the difficulties of language: Perry's knowledge of Spanish was inadequate to the occasion, and the interrogator had only sparse English. When Perry, in growing anxiety for himself and Halfhyde, tried to speak of guns and ammunition aboard the *Taronga Park*, and demanded that a message be sent to the British Embassy, his words were brushed aside as an irrelevance. No-one was concerned about that. There was a murder enquiry and Perry was at the heart of it.

* * *

Aboard the *Taronga Park* the resources of the engineer's stores and workshop had proved as rudimentary as Halfhyde had believed they would. Captain Good, now suffering in his sister's home in Balmain, had not overspent his money as sale and retirement loomed; and Halfhyde's finance base was a shallow one. In any case no master would have anticipated that his Second Engineer would run amok and smash the machinery . . .

There was murder in Higgins' face when the reports reached him. 'What are we expected to do?' he demanded. 'Wallow around in the Doldrums till we all die from starvation?'

Halfhyde shrugged. 'You brought it on yourself, Higgins, though it's pointless to recriminate now. We have to accept it, and hope for a tow.'

'That's too dangerous—'

'For you, yes! It so happens there's no alternative, and we must hope that a ship will overhaul us. But even so, we can't expect a tow all the way to Queenstown—'

'Where, then?'

Again Halfhyde shrugged. 'The nearest port with repair facilities.'

'And that is?'

'The Cape Verde Islands, if the Portuguese will offer their facilities. We're in five degrees north latitude at this moment, and that means a tow of around seven hundred and fifty miles to Sao Vicente and Porto Grande.'

Higgins paced the bridge. 'How long a delay, in Porto Grande?'

'That's impossible to say. But it's not important. The fact of a tow is vital. It's our only chance. If the first ship we sight is bound south, then we shall have to settle for Recife in Brazil, a longer tow and in the wrong direction. But that, too, will have to be accepted if necessary.' Halfhyde looked aloft at the two black-painted canvas spheres hoisted to the foreyard in indication that the ship was not under control . . . in more ways than one, he reflected bitterly. He turned to the Second Mate. 'Mr Foster, I'm going below to my cabin. I'm to be informed immediately a ship is sighted and in the meantime you'll be ready to hoist a flag signal asking for assistance.'

'Aye, aye, sir.'

Halfhyde went down the ladder. The ship had a worse feel than ever now. Silent and drifting beneath a tropic sun, no movement of air across her decks, no air to be scooped up by the

99

bell-mouthed ventilators, high humidity and a hostile crew: it was a vicious first voyage for an owner-master. Savagely Halfhyde cursed his luck as he paced the deck outside his cabin, backwards and forwards, his mind roving over all the possibilities. A tow might well be dangerous for Porteous Higgins but there was no guarantee that it would bring any comfort to Halfhyde and the ship either. Higgins had an iron control and too many men and he could still ride it out. There was no need for any physical contact between the *Taronga Park* and any ship that might offer a tow north or south; that ship need never suspect anything. Halfhyde and his few loyal hands would still be under duress. They would all be closely watched, given no chance to shout a message across as the towing vessel manoeuvred into position. That was obvious. There was just one possible hope: that Porteous Higgins had no knowledge of flag hoists, of the International Code of signals at sea. It could be taken that none of his paid traitors would have that knowledge: the fo'c'sle crowd aboard any merchant ship was an ignorant one and even those who could read and write were very few. Only the officers had the knowledge, and Foster was loyal.

Something might yet be done.

Halfhyde felt stifled by the terrible steamy haze that hung over everything, stifled by the frustration of inactivity and sheer helplessness as the ship drifted. There was sticky moisture everywhere, as bad as a vapour bath. The day wore on, slowly; no ship was sighted. The sea stood utterly empty until a sailing vessel was sighted and Halfhyde went to the bridge, more as a formality than anything else. The sailing vessel was as much at the mercy of the Doldrums as was the *Taronga Park*; the two ships had simply come closer, come within sight of each other, as a result of the drift. In any case a sailing vessel would be hard put to it to offer a tow of any distance even when a wind sprang up. But the opportunity offered and Halfhyde, ready prepared, took it: he managed to pass a scrap of paper to Foster, who could work it out at his leisure, and formulate a flag hoist that would tell another ship's master just enough of the truth.

That night the weather changed abruptly, as so often in the

Doldrums: a violent squall came with torrential rain that lashed down and set up a drumming on the hatch covers, lightning criss-crossed the lowering sky, flickering around the masts and yards as it found the ship's conductor, bringing close thunder-claps that seemed about to burst men's ears with a fury of sound. The whole ship rattled and shook to the thunder and at times seemed to be on fire from the continual jags of lightning. Water was flung across her decks to join the teeming rain. On the bridge, Halfhyde and Gaboon stood isolated as though on some storm-lashed moor like Macbeth's witches. After the squall there was a brooding period of calm before another one hit; when the dawn came up the sailing-ship had vanished, no doubt having taken advantage of the wind to resume her passage and pick up the regularity of the north-east trades. Once again, the sea was empty. Halfhyde, after having been relieved by Foster for the middle watch from midnight to 4 am, was back again on the bridge. Butcher came up with breakfast: coffee and porridge, nothing else. Food was being conserved against the future's uncertainty. They might have a need even to cook and eat the very rats and cockroaches before long. Halfhyde reflected grimly that Higgins might even consider cannibalism once all the food was gone. But surely a ship must come . . .

* * *

A rough hand was shaking Perry's shoulder. He came awake, startled out of another revolving nightmare. 'What is it?'

'Wake, you.'

Perry sat up; it was night and an oil lamp in the man's hand gave yellow light to show up the walls of the cell and the opened door, where another man stood.

A uniformed policeman said, 'You go to Osorno.'

'What for?'

'It is orders. For your trial later. Get up, and come.'

The man bent and released the ankle irons. Perry got to his feet and was marched out of the door, feeling groggy enough to need support. He was taken through an office and out into the street, where a closed horse-drawn vehicle waited. His two guards accompanied him into the vehicle's interior and sat one on either side of him. Each man carried a drawn revolver; and once they were settled one of them produced a pair of handcuffs which were locked on to Perry's wrists. The horse was jerked into movement and the carriage rolled away, lurching and groaning its way along the rough street and out of Puerto Montt northwards for Osorno, some seventy miles distant. The armed guards chattered to each other in Spanish but no word was addressed to Perry. It was a fearful drive over an apology for a road. Perry's anxieties mounted; but at least he was going in the right direction, and perhaps at Osorno there would be somebody in authority who would listen to him.

TEN

Halfhyde's speaking-tube whined at him. He woke at once and took up the tube. It was Foster. A steamship was coming up from astern.

'Bend on the flag hoist,' Halfhyde said. He pulled on shirt and trousers and climbed to the bridge. There was an altercation in progress, and Foster was looking flushed.

'What's the trouble?' Halfhyde asked.

Higgins answered. 'There will be no flag signal, Halfhyde.'

'I say there will—'

'No.' Higgins brought out his revolver and aimed it at Halfhyde. The man at the wheel, one of Higgins' men as Halfhyde knew only too well, stood ready to assist if there was trouble. Higgins said, 'You already have the signal showing the ship not under control. The other ship will close us, and you will call across. If you say any more than the bare facts of the breakdown in the engine – without details of how it happened, just that the engine is out of action – then you'll regret it.' He grinned. 'Gaboon is below with the girl. He has his orders.'

'You'll not sacrifice your hostage at this stage, Higgins.'

'Don't put that fragile hope to the test,' Higgins said.

Halfhyde clenched his fists in fury. Higgins had all the answers and always seemed to keep one jump ahead; but there was nothing to be done about that now. The ship was coming up fast and it was clear that Higgins would be proved right in his assumption: the NUC balls were magnet enough for any shipmaster. When the two vessels were within hailing distance, the master of the overtaking ship used his megaphone.

'What ship?'

'*Taronga Park* out of Sydney for Queenstown,' Halfhyde called back. 'And you?'

'*Barry Island* of Cardiff, out of Valparaiso for Barry Roads, Captain Evan Thomas.'

The voice was very Welsh. Halfhyde called back, 'Can you assist me? My engine's broken down, a job for a dockyard.'

'I have a good engineer, man.'

'No,' Higgins said, his voice hard. 'I'm having no-one come aboard. Tell him that, Halfhyde.'

Halfhyde swallowed his anger and took up his megaphone again. 'It's beyond an engineer's capacity. What I'm asking for is a tow, Captain.'

'A tow is it? Where to?'

'Porto Grande.'

'Porto Grande, I see, yes.' There was a pause. 'There will be a question of salvage money, of course.' There was another silence while Captain Thomas consulted with his First Mate. 'I suggest a thousand pounds, Captain,' he shouted at last.

'Five hundred,' Halfhyde called back.

'It is a long way, a very long way, to Porto Grande,' Captain Thomas shouted across. 'A tow will cause me delay, and my owners, Smith's of Cardiff, will not like that, you know, man.'

Higgins said angrily, 'Offer him what he asks.'

Halfhyde scowled and turned back towards the *Barry Island*. In all truth the price made little odds unless he lived to meet the bills; and currently the most pressing problem was to win through. But he haggled a little more; and eventually the price was agreed at eight hundred pounds to be settled in Porto Grande by a bond to be drawn up before the British Consul. Higgins didn't like that but had to accept it; he could no doubt be relied upon to find a way around any visit ashore by Halfhyde. The price agreed, the *Barry Island* manoeuvred ahead of the *Taronga Park* and Halfhyde sent the Second Mate down to the fo'c'sle to prepare to take the tow from the Welshman. A heaving-line was sent across from the towing vessel and a grass line was brought aboard, backed up by two heavy towing hawsers that were made fast aboard the *Taronga Park*. When

Halfhyde indicated that he was ready, Captain Thomas moved ahead dead slow to take up the slack. The towing pendant came up, bar taut and dripping, then eased back to lie safely with its middle section beneath the water as the *Taronga Park* moved forward to the pull.

'Careful watching, Mr Foster,' Halfhyde said. 'If the tow lifts clear of the water, warn the *Barry Island* without delay.' He stayed for some while on the bridge, watching out himself. But the weather so far was still a flat calm that should give little trouble as long as it lasted. He estimated that it would take seven days at their slow speed to enter Porto Grande; the weather could change in seven days, but Halfhyde's reading of the sky told him that it should last fair, though the oily calm would vanish once they entered the trades.

They made steady progress thereafter and Higgins began to relax in his manner though not in his overall vigilance. His mind, Halfhyde fancied, would be busy now on ensuring that things went his way while the ship was in the Cape Verde Islands. As to the length of time they would need to spend in port undergoing repairs, that was still one of the imponderables. It all depended on how fast the Portuguese could be persuaded to work; the actual job, assuming spares were available, should not in fact take long. And it was likely enough that Higgins would be greasing a few of the important palms, even likely that he had good contacts in Porto Grande who would ease things for him and ensure that the ship's cargo was not called into question. On the face of it, there was no reason why it should be – unless Halfhyde could find some way of opening his mouth in regard to its true nature. And if he did that, he would need to be very sure he was speaking to the right person and not someone bribed in the meantime by Porteous Higgins. If only the port was to be British . . . but Higgins would never have entered in that case. He would have found it safer to accept Captain Evan Thomas' offer of his engineer's assistance.

* * *

They came into the north-east trades and a fresh wind that

lifted some of the depression as clean air was blown through the ventilators and the close heat vanished. The sea broke into waves with a fine spray blown from their tops; but the tow remained relatively unaffected as they came closer to the Cape Verde Islands.

Halfhyde had a feeling, a seaman's instinct, that his first estimation had been wrong and that a blow was coming. There was a drop in the barometric pressure, little enough, but indicative of possibly more to come; and the temperature, too, was showing a small decline. Later as they came north, further into the trades, the sky changed: cloud came up on the horizon, a long, low line to the north-east.

'We're in for it, Mr Foster,' Halfhyde said as he came to the bridge. 'Go below and see all gear secured.' As the Second Mate went down the ladder, Halfhyde studied the approaching cloud bank for a while then turned to the chart. By dead reckoning from the last noon sight, the Cape Verde Islands now lay around twelve hours ahead. If the weather struck hard and failed to moderate before that time, their ability to enter would be in doubt. Halfhyde, as the weight of wind grew steadily, watched the tow-line in increasing anxiety. It was beginning to lift regularly from the water, coming bar taut; aboard the *Barry Island* hands had been sent aft to pay out more rope so as to increase the weight and hold down the tow; but this didn't seem to be helping the situation much.

Higgins, hunched against the fore rail of the bridge, turned round to face Halfhyde. 'Is the tow going to take the strain?' he asked.

'If the wind increases much more, I doubt it.'

'What then?'

Halfhyde shrugged. 'Either the tow will part, or Captain Thomas will cast it off.'

'And us?'

'There's nothing we can do about it. We drift – that's all!'

'How do we get into Porto Grande?'

'We won't.'

Higgins drummed his fists on the rail. 'Surely they have tugs, steam tugs that they can send out?'

106

'No doubt they have, but they need a sight of us first. A lot depends on exactly where the weather worsens to the point that ends the tow from one cause or the other. And that's in the hands of God, not mine – or yours either.'

Higgins swore and turned away again to face for'ard. Halfhyde stared at his back. Higgins was facing a possible end to his dream now; but if so, then all of them were facing an end to their own dreams as well. They all faced death, in fact – and if death came not to himself but to his ship, then Halfhyde faced the end of his just-begun career as a shipowner. He could never sustain the total loss of the *Taronga Park*; the insurance money was problematical. Halfhyde, far from versed as yet in the ways of the commercial world, was unsure of his position to say the least. Always insurers had suspicious minds; any loss led to a searching enquiry, and for all Halfhyde knew the carriage of a cargo mendaciously described in the manifest and the bills of lading might invalidate the insurance protection, the more so if that cargo happened to be guns being run to aid an insurrection. But all this would be academic anyway if they were simply to drift endlessly around the oceans until all hands died . . . Halfhyde caught himself up sharply. Despair was a negative emotion: they had picked up one tow, they could pick up another. And Captain Thomas must surely, if the tow parted or had to be cast off, feel an obligation to stand by until the weather moderated enough for him to take up the tow again, or perhaps to report their predicament to the Portuguese in the Cape Verde Islands. In the meantime they had plenty of searoom; things need not be too black.

Already the wind was coming more strongly and was gusting up to gale force. Halfhyde watched the *Barry Island* through his binoculars; Captain Thomas and his First Mate were staring aft, watching the tow with as much anxiety as himself. The light began to fade from the sky, to make matters worse. By this time, with obviously no more rope available to be paid out aboard the *Barry Island*, the line was almost continually lifted clear of the water and the jerk could be felt as the fo'c'sle rose against it.

'It can't last long now,' Halfhyde said to Foster. The Second Mate, when reporting all secure below, had reported also that the hands were working together, the good and the bad, for the ship's safety, for their own survival. Halfhyde remarked on this now. 'The hands, Mr Foster. They may be acting as seamen first while this lasts, not as Higgins' men – but I wonder how long that'll hold up? If something disastrous comes along, then I fear the knives will be out, each man for himself.'

'You believe we're in real danger, sir?'

Halfhyde nodded. 'Yes, I do. I've a feeling we're steaming into something exceptional in the way of weather. A feeling in my bones, Mr Foster, nothing more, but it's happened to me before.'

'And you've been proved right, sir?'

'Yes. But I've been able to do something about it. This time . . .' He didn't finish the sentence; there was no need. A steamship adrift without power in dirty weather was no-one's idea of safety, any more than was a dismasted windjammer. Halfhyde said crisply, 'Below again, Mr Foster. We have some heavy canvas in the deck store – I'd have used it in the first place if we'd not been in the Doldrums with no wind. Take some of the more experienced hands – O'Dowd and Byers in particular – and break out that canvas. O'Dowd can get to work fashioning a sail of some sort for rigging from the fore yard. Once that's done we can see if we can fit out the main as well. It's worth a try.'

Foster turned away for the ladder. Just as he did so the ship was shaken by a violent gust; the head was thrown off hard to port, the tow-line gave a heavy, jarring jerk and then fell slack, the inboard end running back through the water until it lay up-and-down, trailing uselessly as the distance between the *Taronga Park* and the *Barry Island* widened.

* * *

It was not only out at sea that dirty weather could strike; Perry, heading north for Osorno, heard the whine of the wind and the pounding of heavy rain on the roof of the carriage. Both wind and rain penetrated the creaking old vehicle, and Perry's guards fiddled uselessly with the window straps in an attempt to keep discomfort out. They muttered and cursed in Spanish;

one of them was looking sick from the terrible motion of the vehicle as it lurched and swayed along the track like a ship at sea. The pace had slowed as though either the horse was weary of effort or the coachman was reluctant to make speed in the prevailing conditions. After a while the carriage came to a halt and Perry heard the man getting down from his box. A thunderous knocking came at the window, and one of the armed guards released the heavy leather strap to let in wind and rain and the anxious face of the coachman.

There was a torrent of words from which Perry gathered that the coach had, unfortunately, left the track. There had been an error of navigation in the darkness – the fault of the so-terrible track, not of the coachman . . . there was no knowing, once the rain turned everything into mud, which was track and which was not. There was an almighty row, the policeman jerked viciously at the strap, almost severing the coachman's nose as the window flew up, and the wretched man climbed back to his box. The carriage started off again, lurching more than ever as the wheels ran into deep ruts and climbed out of them again with an immense effort on the part of the horse.

Obviously, they were now proceeding by guess and by God; probably in as straight a line as possible for Osorno, or the coachman's concept of where Osorno lay. Perry gloomed; he knew he was being overtaken by events, that it was unlikely now that he would ever get his message through to Santiago. He might well be going the right way, however slowly; but his hopes of getting an audience in Osorno were diminishing the more he thought about the prospect. The authorities in Osorno would be as impervious as those in Puerto Montt. He was already branded as a murderer, and no-one paid attention to murderers who could be presumed to wish to procrastinate, to invent any story, however unlikely, that might delay their inevitable end. Perry was uncertain whether or not Chile sanctioned capital punishment, but presumed that it did. Perry had no wish to die; but if he had to, then he would die the less reluctantly if first he had carried out his duty and his orders. There was a stubbornness in him that made him determined to do this whatever finally happened to himself.

There was a filthy fug inside the carriage: one of the armed policemen had for some while past been smoking small, cheap cigars of an appalling ferocity, taking no notice of the appeals of his green-faced companion. The stench sickened even Perry. Outside, the weather was worsening, so was the track. It felt as though they were driving over rocks; when a little later one of the leaf springs gave up the ghost, the discomfort grew: the carriage proceeded on its way with a heavy list to starboard, so that Perry lay hard up against the cigar smoker. It was not long after that when the end came. There was a high, fearful whinney from ahead and a yell of terror from the coachman and on the heels of the yell came a dropping sensation, a feeling of weightlessness that ended abruptly in an appalling crash. The carriage split open, all down one side, and as the vehicle toppled Perry was flung clear through an aperture from which the door had been wrenched during the fall. He landed, still handcuffed, in a patch of soft mud. Nearby in the flickering light of a tallow lantern that had survived he saw the coachman, lying very still with his head at a curious angle. The man's neck, Perry believed, was broken.

He scrambled to his feet. He appeared to be intact; the coach, as he now saw, had skidded off the track and fallen down a bank, to fetch up on a bare, rocky outcrop. Perry believed there were trees beyond, the fringe of a forest reaching out towards the track. The horse was screaming but not moving anything except for one leg. Broken back, three broken legs? The screaming seemed to curdle his blood. He took a deep breath and cautiously approached the coach. No-one emerged, but he heard groans.

He heaved himself up, a hard job with his handcuffed wrists, and looked down through the doorless hole. One of the policemen was, he thought, dead: possibly a broken neck like the coachman. The other, the groaning one, was in delirium. He was the one with the key to the handcuffs. Perry let himself down into the dark interior. Groping around, he found the man's belt and a bunch of keys on a ring. This he managed to remove; he tried the keys. The fourth one fitted. Freed of the cuffs, Perry felt for and found one of the revolvers. Clambering out of the coach again, he put the gun to the horse's head and fired. The screaming stopped.

Half tempted to retain the revolver, he decided not to. If he were picked up with a police revolver in his possession things would go badly for him. He threw it back into the coach and then moved away, anywhere that would take him into the night's thickness and hide him. When he had gone perhaps three or four hundred yards he saw a sudden glare casting light from behind, and he turned.

The coach was ablaze. That tallow lantern . . . it couldn't be seen now. It could have come adrift and fallen straight down through the gap in the carriage side. There was rain, yes – but basically the woodwork was as dry as tinder. Perry instinctively took a few paces back towards the carriage; one of the guards had been alive. But even as he moved he knew it was useless. The carriage was already well ablaze, flames shooting, wreathed in smoke and crackling sparks. He turned away. By using his seaman's instinct for the north point of the compass, using the sun's position when dawn came, he might reach Osorno. There was no certainty but it was all he could do. And so far as was humanly possible he had to remain anonymous, unseen. There could be no asking for directions if he came upon some sort of habitation. That fire had been fortuitous; it just might obscure the fact that only two bodies were in the carriage. If so, and it was a long shot undoubtedly, he might be presumed charred with the others. That was worth making use of.

He stumbled on through the night, through clinging mud and over rocks that on occasions threw him to the ground. He was still moving on when the rain stopped and the first faint streaks of dawn lit the sky and gave him a direction. Soon he was climbing, and meeting less mud. Another hour and he found a mountain stream, rushing in full torrent down into the valley, past the lower slopes where he was walking. He stopped, feeling dizzy with weariness and hunger. He collapsed to the ground and was asleep by the water's edge within seconds. As he slept sheep came by, emerging from their rough shelter as the day became less turbulent, seeking sparse grass to munch.

The sun shone through gaps in the cloud, bringing a touch of warmth.

* * *

During the night hours of that day Perry walked circumspectly into Osorno. On waking by the stream he had stripped as he had done back in the entry to Reloncavi Bay, had washed his body and his clothing in the clear water, and had then laid out the clothing to dry in the mounting heat of the sun. Finding more water at intervals subsequently, he had kept clean. His thirst had been assuaged by the stream water, his hunger was being held at bay by his having eaten some wild-growing edibles outside the town – berries, dates, beans.

Now his target was the railway station. There might for all he knew be telegraph facilities in Osorno, but to approach a telegraph office was too much of a risk: he was a fugitive who wished to leave no spoor behind him, and in any case it was ridiculous to suppose that any official would accept a message for the British Embassy from a penniless, unshaven vagabond.

Perry asked no directions; he skirted the main part of the town until he picked up the railway line running down from Santiago. The rest was all plain sailing; the station was an open affair, no platform, into which anyone could wander at will. Having found his target, Perry went to ground again, choosing a derelict, roofless building from which he could watch not only the railway line but all avenues of approach as well. He had no idea how often the trains ran; patience might be needed yet. But it was a fair wager that the town's only line must run to Santiago. Once the train came in, he would have a fair chance of boarding it clandestinely as it steamed out again. No money meant no ticket; his troubles would be far from over unless he could sneak away unseen from the station in the capital, which would be better supervised than this one.

Once again dawn came up.

Perry had resisted sleep in the interest of remaining watchful for pursuit or the advent of a train; he had scarcely been able to keep his eyelids apart but, used to long hours on a ship's bridge in bad weather, he had done no more than drift off for seconds at a time. Now, in the dawn, as he looked out from his cover, he saw a man in the distance, back towards the railway station. This man was coming closer, carrying a knapsack. He had the down-at-heel look of a harmless tramp. Nevertheless, Perry sank back behind the remnants of the walls.

* * *

Aboard the *Taronga Park*, the canvas had been brought out and fashioned into two makeshift sails by O'Dowd who, though not a sailmaker, had some knowledge of the craft and possessed a sailmaker's palm among his seagoing kit. When hauled up to the fore yard, the canvas had some effect in steadying the ship though it seemed, at any rate in current conditions, not enough to give her any way through the water.

In the meantime Captain Thomas had taken the *Barry Island* round to port and had come up to lie off to leeward of the helpless vessel. He could be seen shouting through his megaphone but the strong wind blew his words away. When he realized that he was unheard, he began signalling in morse with a not-very-efficient lamp.

Halfhyde read off his signal. 'He's intending to keep us company, Mr Foster.' He gave a harsh laugh. 'I wonder for how far!'

Foster suggested, 'Until he's sure of the salvage money, sir!'

'Very likely, but we mustn't be ungenerous in our thoughts. He could be our salvation, never mind salvage! At the least he might be persuaded to enter Porto Grande on our behalf, and ask for steam tugs. That is, if the weather moderates.' Currently it was worsening. Huge waves fell on the decks and the whole ship vibrated to their weight; with the current inability to get way on her the one thing that might enable her to steer, or, failing that, to keep her heading into the wind by virtue of its presence, the jury-ripped sail. If properly handled by orders from the bridge correctly carried out by the seamen manning the sheets leading down from the eyelets in the four corners of the canvas, it just might be enough.

But fate was against the *Taronga Park*. As more men struggled at the mainmast aft of the bridge in an attempt to send up and secure the second sail, that at the foremast was taken by a sudden freakish shift of the wind, flapped violently, dragged the starboard-side rope from the hands of the men, flew up into the night and with a whipping, tearing sound, burst free from the yard and vanished away over the plunging bows.

Halfhyde yelled out to the hands at the mainmast.

'Take it down – bring the sail for'ard, and make it quick if you don't want to drown!' He turned to the Second Mate. 'Get down there, Mr Foster, and don't waste a second. It'll hold the ship better on the foremast and we've not much time.'

Foster slid down the ladder on the palms of his hands and raced aft. As he went, the ship came round to the weight of the wind and sea, already listing hard to port, pushed over and over by the terrible pounding of the waves, the wind shrieking like a chorus of demons through the rigging. The starboard side of the bridge lifted sharply, sending Halfhyde and Higgins over against the port rail. Higgins looked white and shaken, scared to death in Halfhyde's view. Menacing sounds came from below decks as all manner of gear began moving about. Halfhyde was filled with alarm by this time, knowing the cargo could have shifted; such a dead weight, smashing through the shifting boards to pile up on the lee side of his holds, was going to put the ship in greater jeopardy and might well mean her end. As the decks took an even more pronounced slant the threatening noises grew worse. Now the raging seas were running close below the port side of the bridge. Higgins looked round at Halfhyde, his eyes wide.

'What are you going to do?' he shouted.

'There's nothing to be done now, Higgins.'

'For Christ's sake!'

'This is a hazard of the sea. To attempt to trim the ship by sending men down to move the cargo – that's impossible in the prevailing conditions—'

'But surely—'

'I'm the master, Higgins. I'm the seaman, not you.' Halfhyde was having to shout to make himself heard at all. 'We hope to ride the storm and when we've done that, we shift the hold stowage again and trim the ship. For now, we're helpless.

But the ship's sound basically and there's a chance we shall come through.' Leaning his body backwards against the slant of the bridge, so far back that he was almost at right angles to the guardrail, he peered through the night's thickness with his binoculars, trying to locate the *Barry Island*. If Captain Thomas was still standing by and if, when disaster came, Halfhyde could get a lifeboat away, that boat just might manage to ride it out until the weather moderated, when its crew could be picked up by the Welshman. That seemed to be the one remaining hope and it wasn't a very strong one: to lower a boat without smashing it against the ship's side in such seas would be almost as impossible as trying to sort out the wreckage in the holds.

In the meantime Foster was making a brave but doomed attempt to get his makeshift sail hauled to the fore yard. Men struggled across the wet, slippery deck, moving uphill to the starboard ratlines, taking ropes aloft to haul the canvas up from the well-deck, but once again the shrieking wind took charge. The second piece of canvas followed the first.

This time, it took a man with it. Halfhyde was unable to see who he was. But he caught the tail end of the panic-stricken yell and saw the man topple from the yard, come down hard on the fo'c'sle-head and bounce overboard into the white-topped sea. For a moment the body was seen, head down, riding the crest of a wave and looking as thought it was about to be hurled back inboard. Then it dropped back and vanished as the water sucked away from the ship.

Higgins was staring as if he had witnessed a prophecy of his own end. Halfhyde said, 'You should have confined your dirty work to Australia, Higgins. The sea's a dangerous thing.'

ELEVEN

Perry watched as the unknown man approached his hideout. He might go on past; in any case Perry couldn't move away without being spotted. But the man, as soon became obvious, was making straight for the derelict building.

He came in, stopped dead with lifted eyebrows and open mouth when he saw someone else was there. Perry looked back at him; he was plainly a tramp, his clothing worn and shabby, with frayed trouser-ends. His face was seamed and wizened with age and weather, an open-air face with very blue eyes.

He said, '*Buenos dias, Señor.*'

'*Buenos dias,*' Perry responded in an execrable accent.

The man laughed. 'You sound and look English,' he said.

'So do you.'

'I am! So well met, fellow Englishman, however unpropitious the surroundings. Have you as it were taken to the road, friend?'

'Not exactly,' Perry said.

'Ha!' The man put down his knapsack and sat on the ruination of the floor, leaning back against a crumbling wall. 'Well, I'll ask no questions, it doesn't do. As for me, I'm what the Americans call a bum. I live on the generosity of other people, and believe me it's a thin enough living. But I like it – I like the freedom. The freedom to come and go as I please, the freedom not to work when I don't want to. Now and again, of course, financial pressures force me into a little endeavour – odd jobs before moving on. No doubt you find the same necessity?'

'I've worked hard,' Perry said carefully, 'all my life.'

'A seaman by the look of you – don't tell me, I'm sure I'm right. Missed your ship down south, I'll wager.'

'Something like that.'

'Not a true blue bum, not one of the fraternity.' The man sighed. 'Ah well, we can't all be the same. I expect you're hungry?' He didn't wait for an answer; he opened up his knapsack and brought out a hunk of bread and some very stale cheese, together with a knife. He cut off a piece of the bread and handed it to Perry with a segment of cheese. Perry thanked him and ate hungrily and gratefully. When he had eaten the man asked him if he was waiting for the train for Santiago.

'How did you know?' Perry asked in surprise.

The man waved a hand airily. 'Because I am, too. And this is a handy spot – and as I've already elucidated, you're a seaman, and Valparaiso, which is not so far from Santiago, is a seaman's paradise in many ways – but you'll know that, of course. It's the very place to look for a ship bound for home. Another point: the trains run there from Santiago.' He paused. 'I'm making another assumption. You've no money.'

'It was stolen,' Perry said.

'Ah yes. The world over, seamen are easy prey. Their wants are too well known – women and liquor first, if I may say so without giving offence. Once ashore, they're lost and are taken advantage of. But don't worry . . . I have no money either. That will not preclude us taking the train, which is due into the station in two hours' time. Obviously, your intention was to hide yourself away. So is mine. But I'm more experienced than you, so you'll now have a much better chance. How very fortunate we met, my dear fellow!' He cut off some more bread and cheese, sharing it once again with Perry. 'I wonder . . . shall we exchange names? I'll not press, but it makes life easier—'

'Perry.' The man seemed genuine, and a decent sort, with a straight look and honest eyes.

'Thank you, Mr Perry. Mine is D'Arcy. Algernon David D'Arcy, sent down from Cambridge in sixty-one, the year the Confederates fired upon Fort Sumter and began the American

Civil War, not that there was any connection.' D'Arcy flicked a speck of dirt from his deplorable coat sleeve. 'War was not my forte. Mine was drink and no desire at all to work. I have overcome the former from force of circumstance, but not the latter.'

'I see,' Perry said.

D'Arcy shrugged. 'I doubt if you really do, but never mind. Your sort and mine are poles apart, of course, but I have a feeling we shall be friends so long as we're together. The train, by the way, takes two days to reach Santiago so from now on we shall curb our appetites. With care I have enough food and water for two people.'

'I'll be an encumbrance—'

D'Arcy held up a hand peremptorily. 'By no means. You are my guest. Despite all, I have not forgotten my manners.'

* * *

Gaboon came to the bridge. Clutching at everything he could lay hands on for safety, he made a slow approach to Higgins. Grunts emerged from his mouth but his communication with his master was, as Halfhyde had seen before, by means of a kind of sign language. Higgins got the purport of the message and turned towards Halfhyde.

He said, 'Water's coming in aft, in the engineers' accommodation. The girl's cabin.'

'Is she all right?'

Higgins nodded. 'Yes. She's all right, the cabin isn't. The port's under water and leaking badly.'

'Tell Gaboon to bring her up to my cabin, Higgins.'

'He—'

'At once.' Halfhyde's voice was a whiplash. The exigencies of the sea were putting him firmly back in a position of authority and Higgins didn't argue further. Halfhyde wondered fleetingly if this was the time to make an all-out attempt at re-establishing total control of the ship, but he knew inside himself that it was not. No weapons and almost all his crew against him still – and for the moment at least the ship's safety must come first. For now the fo'c'sle crowd was working together; that truce must not be shattered. The ship was in considerable danger from the sea; if she foundered it wouldn't matter a tinker's curse who held the upper hand.

During the night Halfhyde had picked up the steaming lights, red, green and white, of the *Barry Island*: she was still in company, lying well off to leeward but giving the comforting knowledge of her presence. Now, as the sky lightened a little, she could be seen dipping and plunging and lifting again to the mountainous South Atlantic seas but riding well enough. Captain Evan Thomas was not suffering from a shifted cargo and his ship was taking it comparatively easily. Once the gale had passed, the hands aboard the *Taronga Park* were going to face a daunting task. It was never easy to shift cargo at sea and this time there must be an appalling mess below. Halfhyde believed also that he had drifted well to westward of his intended course, blown right off track, helplessly, by the relentless wind and the scend of the sea. This process was still continuing and looked like doing so for a long while yet; there was no sign whatever of any lift in the weather. And Halfhyde had no current means of checking his position to establish the distance of the drift. There had been no stars and no moon, and now there was no sun visible; and likewise there was no horizon. His sextant lay useless, as would that of Captain Thomas aboard the *Barry Island*.

By now the port bulwarks were dipping beneath the sea all along the ship; she was riding with a list of some forty-five degrees, teetering on the danger mark, the point of no return when a heavier-than-usual gust of wind or shock of sea sweeping down on her lifted starboard side would send her right over to capsize and fill with pounding tons of water that would hold her bottom upwards for a time until she went down with all of her crew that hadn't jumped in time.

Jumped into what?

Death by drowning, or by being hurled back against the sides and upperworks of the sinking ship. The sea was a thing of immense power; there was nothing made yet by man that could match its strength. Halfhyde believed he was watching the harshest manifestation of that terrible power that he had ever seen. Typhoons in the China Sea, hurricanes in the West Indies, lashing gales in the North Atlantic and the Great Australian Bight – he had seen them all during his Naval service for the Queen, but there had never been anything to equal this for ferocity and duration. It was as though heaven itself had it in for Porteous Higgins and his schemes, but for some reason intended the innocent to suffer with him and the dreadful Gaboon. There was no extension of mercy, no flicker of hope offered.

As Halfhyde watched, feeling every jar of his ship as a blow to his own body, as a personal assault, he saw the line of the sea encroach still further. No longer were the port bulwarks making a brief appearance as the sea drained away; now they were permanently under and the water was coming up the deck itself to lap the hatch coamings. He stared in helpless horror. He caught Higgins' half-demented eye: Higgins was trembling like a leaf.

Halfhyde laughed, a hard, humourless sound. 'Your wretched armoury, Higgins . . . it'll be full of salt water by now, and useless till the guns are cleaned one by one!'

Higgins drew a hand across his face. 'There'll be time for that once they're ashore in Ireland.'

'If ever we get there.'

'You think we'll not?'

'Yes. That is what I think, Higgins.'

'What about our lives, then?'

Halfhyde shrugged, sensing the man's fear. Higgins, his voice high, screamed back at him. 'Why don't you do something . . . abandon ship at least?'

'I've said before, you're no seaman. Who could get a boat away in this?'

'But if it gets worse—'

'It's too late already, Higgins. It was too late the moment we took that list, with the weather as it was. No-one could have foreseen that, and only cowards abandon too soon.'

Higgins, pulling his heavy body along the bridge rail, took a step towards him. There was a red glint in his eye. His free hand went inside his oilskin and came out with his revolver aimed at

Halfhyde. He was mouthing something, but a gust of wind took his words away. Halfhyde stood his ground. He shouted, 'Have a care, Higgins. You're going to need me to save your rotten skin! Just keep that in mind.'

Livid, Higgins lifted the revolver higher. Just as he squeezed the trigger Halfhyde let gravity take him. Down the sloping deck of the bridge, he dropped on Higgins. There was a report and a flash; the bullet sped past Halfhyde's ear. He made a grab for the arm and forced it back, down towards the rail. As the arm was wrenched hard over the metal, Higgins let go of the revolver and it dropped into the sea.

'Right,' Halfhyde said in satisfaction. 'Now you're going to wish you'd stayed nice and safe in Sydney, Mr Porteous Higgins!'

Holding the thick neck with one hand, keeping his feet with difficulty on the plunging, listed deck, he smashed his right fist hard into the heavy face, again and again. The flesh began to pulp. Halfhyde was still smashing hard when he felt a blow in his kidneys and heard Gaboon's grunting sounds close to his ear.

* * *

In Osorno, they heard the train in the distance. There was a long-drawn hoot and soon the engine came into view, antiquated and surrounded by clouds of steam and black smoke. It was a long train – fourteen coaches that appeared to be half empty, passing into the station with a good deal of clanking and jerking as the brakes were applied.

D'Arcy had said the train would remain three hours in the station before making its way back to Santiago along the single-track line. 'Plenty of time, Mr Perry,' he observed, hands folded across a lean stomach. He was a thin and wiry man, very well preserved for his age, which Perry reckoned must be close on sixty. 'Let us rest while we may.' Already he had told Perry what their mode of transport would be: not a comfortable one but beggars could not be choosers. 'Never could. I chose to be a beggar, you see. It has its drawbacks, one must admit – but still! My father maintained a carriage and pair, but today we travel, you and I, Mr Perry, in a mobile sheep pen, which will leave Osorno empty but is liable to be occupied *en route*, which will be tiresome but has to be borne—'

'Won't we be seen getting in?' Perry asked.

'Oh, no.' D'Arcy waved a hand indifferently. 'Because we'll not board in the station, you see. Soon we shall leave this abode and head a little way north to where there's an incline and a tunnel and – rather important – a forest. That's where we embark, while the train is moving only slowly.'

'And when the sheep come aboard?'

D'Arcy smiled. 'Ah! Then we move out, but only temporarily. We shall climb over the side before the embarkation point is reached, and hang above the buffers. A certain amount of agility is needed, of course, but if I can do it, and I can, so can a younger man. Then, when the train moves out again, we resume more comfortable quarters, sharing them with poor animals consigned to the slaughter-houses of Santiago.'

Perry said dourly, 'It sounds a nasty way to travel.'

'Yes, and it is. But if you wish to reach your destination . . .' D'Arcy shrugged and said no more. It was obvious he was well accustomed to such journeys; he went on to tell Perry that his ultimate destination was the United States of America, a very long journey indeed, north through Chile and Peru, Colombia, Panama, Mexico . . . really, the journey from Osorno to Santiago was a mere bagatelle, child's play. 'The USA's worth it all,' he said, still leaning comfortably back against the wall. 'They know how to treat bums there. Always a crust at the very least, especially if you're English. The accent, you know. It intrigues them. The voice of an English gentleman coming from such an unlikely source—'

'I always heard,' Perry interrupted, 'that they had no time for bums?'

'Well, I confess there's a difference between a bum and a hobo. When making my reconnaissance I always indicate my willingness to work for my sustenance, thus becoming, in fact, a hobo. But still an English one.'

Perry nodded. 'I wonder you've never lost your accent, Mr D'Arcy.'

'Only very common people do that. Oneself, one *never* acquires a colonial twang however long since one was last at home.'

D'Arcy went on to say that they would not leave their hiding place immediately; the walk to their embarkation point would take little more than an hour. They would not, he said, be remarked; they were no more scruffy in their appearance than the majority of Osorno's population and cleaner than some. The train would be carrying a very mixed bag and it was likely enough that they would not be the only human occupants of the sheep pen. The railway authorities were well enough aware that free use was being made of their rolling stock but they were mostly inclined to accept it as a fact of life and only occasionally did they mount a show of zeal, make a search, and belabour the miscreants as they fled. 'So long as one is not obtrusive . . . so long as one doesn't too openly flout them, if you follow, Mr Perry. It's a question of face, as the Chinese have it. To illustrate: my father used not to allow his gardeners to smoke while working, but never pressed the point so long as the man concerned took pains to conceal his pipe on my father's approach.'

Perry understood that; any First Mate who wished to run a happy ship knew as well as D'Arcy's father when to turn a blind eye. There was much poverty in Chile, and ill-paid railwaymen came from the same class as the peasantry . . . in due course Perry set off with D'Arcy, making for the forest-clad incline at the tunnel's mouth.

* * *

Higgins had pulled himself up the sloping deck while Gaboon's gross body held Halfhyde pinned against the rail. Not for long: Halfhyde brought a knee up, sharp and hard. An animal sound of agony came from Gaboon and he moved back a little, doubling up. Halfhyde brought him upright again with a blow to the chin, and the hairy form went backwards, fell, slid across the deck and fetched up in a heap against the rail. From there, eyes blazing, he brought out a revolver. He fired; there was a shout of anger from Higgins. The bullet took Halfhyde in the flesh of his left upper arm, spun him round with the impact. He gripped the bridge rail, saving himself from going over the side. Gaboon dragged himself upright, his gaze fixed on Halfhyde's face.

'Hold it, Gaboon!' Higgins yelled, down wind. Blood was streaming from his nose and one eye was closed. 'Later – *not now*! Give me that gun, Gaboon.'

He moved towards Gaboon, who still held the revolver aimed at Halfhyde. If Halfhyde made one move the man would fire: so much Halfhyde read in his eyes. Higgins, moving fast now, reached Gaboon and wrenched at the gun. After a moment's hesitation Gaboon let go with a bad grace; common sense had penetrated the bone of his head. But he was not going to forget; and he was scarcely the forgiving sort.

Higgins turned to Halfhyde. He said savagely, 'We need you – for now. The time'll come when we don't. Just remember that.'

'You repeat yourself,' Halfhyde snapped. They stared at each other. Higgins turned as someone was heard coming up the ladder.

The Second Mate appeared, took in the scene quickly. He said, 'Your arm, sir—'

'I shall survive, Mr Foster. How are things below?'

'We're taking water, sir, but the pumps are keeping pace so far. I reckon if we don't go further over we'll come through. I believe the wind's a little less heavy now, sir.'

'Barely noticeably, but at least it's no longer worsening.'

'No, sir.' Foster paused. 'I'll take over, sir. You're losing a lot of blood. Miss Penn's in your cabin. I think you should go below at once, sir.'

Halfhyde said impatiently, 'I'm perfectly all right.'

'I hope so, sir. But there's not many of us left now.'

Halfhyde looked at him sharply. What he had said was true; they all had to remain fit and a Captain with, perhaps, a poisoned arm eventually would be of no use to anyone. He gave a brief nod. 'Very well, Mr Foster, I'll go below for some attention. Call me the moment you think it necessary.'

Halfhyde moved for the ladder and went down, not using his

left arm. Both Higgins and Gaboon remained on the bridge, holding on for their lives as the ship heaved and fell again, sluggishly, with a dangerously inert feel to her. From below came a hollow booming as the waves pounded the lifted starboard side. When Halfhyde reached his cabin the girl was full of concern for him, though looking pale and ill herself.

She said, 'I thought I heard a shot. Who was it?'

'Gaboon.' He told her what had taken place. 'How has he been behaving to you, Victoria?'

'Oh, he hasn't bothered me . . . not in the way you mean. But he gives me the bloody creeps just to have him near, just to look at him. That man's really evil.' She gave a toss of her head, throwing off her own troubles. 'Let's have a look at that arm, right?'

He began to take off his oilskin. She helped him to bare the arm. There was a blackened hole, two holes, where the bullet had fortunately passed right through. The flesh around these was bruised and swollen and the arm hurt badly. Victoria asked, 'Got anything antiseptic, have you, Captain?'

'Iodine. In the cupboard.'

She went across, climbing the cabin floor, and found a small bottle. Using a pad of cotton wool, she dabbed away the blood then applied the iodine to the wounds. Halfhyde winced.

'Sorry,' she murmured. The fair hair swept his face; he liked the proximity of her body. She turned away and found a clean shirt in a drawer beneath the bunk, and tore it into strips to fashion a bandage. This she applied tightly to stop the bleeding. 'There,' she said. 'All I can do, I reckon. Wish I was a trained nurse.'

'You're just as good as one,' he said gratefully. 'Thank you. Now I must go back to the bridge.'

'Look,' she said in concern, 'you're bloody near out on your feet. You won't be any good up there if you pass out, will you?'

'The bridge is my place, Victoria.'

She said almost angrily, 'Don't be so bloody daft. Is there anything specific you can do by being up there, anything your Mr Foster can't see to?'

'Emergencies—'

'Right now,' she interrupted, 'you're an emergency yourself. You can't go on for ever. You'd be a liability.'

He snapped an answer at her and turned for the door. As he reached it, he stumbled a little and had to reach out for support. The girl was right there; she put her arms gently about him as a momentary blackness assailed him and he staggered again. She said, 'See what I mean? You're going to stay right here, no bloody argument. A couple of hours' sleep won't sink the ship.'

A minute later he was lying on the bunk, sound asleep, with the girl sitting by his side and looking at him with eyes that had suddenly filled with tears. He was a good man facing appalling luck, troubles that were none of his own making. Porteous Higgins was no good to anyone who came into his orbit and that included herself. One day Porteous Higgins would swing at the end of a rope; that day couldn't come too fast. Victoria thought about Perry. They wouldn't know if he'd got through to the British Embassy until they had made their landfall and either found the Navy waiting or did not. The uncertainty was wicked.

* * *

Perry and D'Arcy sat alone in the sheep truck, which carried plenty of evidence of its function in life. It was difficult to find a clean spot but Perry was far from inclined to cavil at their surroundings, which were carrying them north for Santiago slowly but surely – so far. D'Arcy soon fell asleep, not seeming to be bothered by the rattling and swaying and jerking of bumpers as every now and then the engine altered its pace. Thick smoke swept back on them, chokingly; as they came to tunnels cut through the mountains the air became virtually impossible to breathe, each re-emergence into daylight coming as a benison. Perry was soon sore and bruised from his bodily contact with the woodwork as he tried to hold himself from sliding about the filthy boards. After some hours the train, which at no time had moved very fast, slowed to a crawl and D'Arcy woke.

'The station's not far off,' he said.

'Where the sheep come aboard?'

126

D'Arcy nodded. 'Follow my motions, Mr Perry,' he said. He clambered to his feet, moved to the fore end of the truck and heaved himself up on to the woodwork. Perry did likewise. Immediately ahead of them was the back end of the last coach, swaying from side to side. D'Arcy climbed over, feeling with his feet for the left-hand buffer, keeping a firm grip with his hands on the body of the truck. Perry followed, using the right-hand buffer as a foot-rest. It was easy enough and they rode the last half mile or so reasonably comfortably.

'We'll drop down when the train stops,' D'Arcy said. 'What more natural than to mingle with the passengers whose tickets have already been examined, and stretch our legs?'

Perry agreed. When the train pulled into a rudimentary station, they dropped unseen to the track and walked round the rear of the truck like any fare-paid passenger. A number of people were leaving the train and others were waiting to go aboard. Perry was on the watch for police uniforms; many times whilst waiting for the train in Osorno he had wondered about the fact that there was no search and had come to the conclusion that either he had been right about the effects of the fire or the wreckage had not yet been found at all – this latter was a strong enough probability without a doubt. The coach had been well off the proper track from Puerto Montt and the delay in its arrival in Osorno could have been written off as being due to the rainstorm and the mud or just another familiar manifestation of the Chilean attitude of *mañana*. Whatever the reason, Perry saw no more than one bovine-looking policeman who appeared to be watching over the train's arrival with no particular interest in any of the passengers; currently he was engaged in what appeared from the chuckles and blushes to be a suggestive conversation with a pretty country girl about to board the train. Nevertheless, Perry decided it would be wiser to avoid the policeman's immediate vicinity, and, as they walked towards the engine, he took charge, turning firmly about and marching back the other way.

D'Arcy gave him a knowing look and raised his eyebrows. He had understood. Few words were necessary. 'A trumped-up charge,' Perry said. 'I was, and am, innocent of any crime.'

D'Arcy nodded. 'Your honest face tells me that, Mr Perry.'

'Thank you.'

'And the dagoes are an unreliable lot, mostly liars.' They walked on. After some while the sheep were heard and soon after this they were seen, being shepherded along towards the truck, the tailboard of which was now lowered to the ground to form an embarkation gangway for the animals. There was much baa-ing and a number of sheep dodged leggily aside, making an attempt at escape before they could be urged aboard.

'Now,' D'Arcy said. 'A touch of subterfuge. Nature calls, and will not be denied ... and there is a public lavatory, unsalubrious but handy. Come with me – and remain until the whistle blows. D'you follow, Mr Perry?'

Perry nodded. 'A quick dash at the last moment—'

'And rather than miss the train, we jump in with the sheep.' D'Arcy headed for the ramshackle convenience, which was little more tnan a wooden screen surrounding a hole in the earth. When the whistle blew they waited a little longer until they heard the chug of the engine; then they came out at speed, shouting for the train to stop. It was easily done; as the long line of carriages pulled out, they reached the truck at the end and jumped for the buffers, hung there for a moment regaining their breath, then pulled themselves over the tailboard and dropped down amongst the startled sheep.

TWELVE

The weather had moderated considerably but there was still a fairly nasty sea running, together with a heavy swell. Captain Thomas brought the *Barry Island* in closer and used his megaphone. He called across, asking firstly if he could be of any assistance. He could send hands across to help in righting the *Taronga Park*'s trim. Higgins had anticipated this and now stood behind Halfhyde armed with Gaboon's revolver, ready to ensure obedience to his orders.

'I can manage, Captain,' Halfhyde shouted back. 'I have hands enough, but thank you all the same.'

'It's no trouble,' Captain Thomas answered. 'In the meantime I shall stand by you, don't worry.' He paused, then added, 'Do you know we are some ninety miles to the sou'-west of Porto Grande, Captain?' Halfhyde replied that he was aware of the drift; by this time he had been able to get a sight and fix his ship's position. Thomas called across again. 'When you have trimmed your ship, I shall take up the tow again, and take you all the way into Queenstown. Later we will discuss the terms.' Thomas gave a wave of his megaphone, then turned his back. No notice was taken of further shouts from the *Taronga Park*. Higgins was furiously angry; he had no wish for company when the ship passed inwards of the Fastnet; a repair in Porto Grande would suit him much better.

'Because you have friends there, Higgins, I don't doubt,' Halfhyde said. Higgins didn't answer. As for Halfhyde, he knew that the bill for a tow of such a duration would be astonomical; but he knew, too, that there was no option. His ship was still helpless, utterly at the mercy of the sea and what the sea could do. As a shipmaster he had a responsibility for life and never mind the fact that most of his crew were scum, Higgins' men. He would be forced to accept whatever terms Captain Thomas decided to ask. And ask was scarcely the word; Halfhyde was in the Welshman's hands unless and until some other willing ship hove in sight on a homeward track and thus made bargaining possible. Here again, however, he was unsure of his ground: Her Majesty's ships gave an officer no experience of commercial practice, and Halfhyde didn't know whether or not a ship that had already got its lines aboard what amounted to a derelict had by that *fait accompli* staked an irreversible claim. Foster, when consulted, was himself uncertain, but tended to believe that such was indeed the case. There might, he said, be ways round it.

'Such as?' Halfhyde asked.

'Well, sir, the tow could be slipped . . . at night, say, and put down to—'

'You suggest I tell lies, Mr Foster?'

'Not quite lies, sir—'

'Then what?' Halfhyde's voice was cold. 'I do not tell lies, Mr Foster, never have, never shall. Nor do I throw a fellow captain's assistance back in his teeth even though he has a fine eye to the main chance! If I strike a bargain and there is no decent and accepted way out of it under maritime practice, then that bargain stays. To do less would be to put myself on the same level as vermin like Higgins.'

Foster apologized, looking somewhat shame-faced. Halfhyde left him on watch and went below to pace his deck. Like the girl earlier, he thought and worried about Perry. But there should be no need to worry; Perry's mission was simple and straightforward enough and the Embassy in Santiago would be bound to act the moment he reported, and cable lines would be fast. It could well be that at this moment a squadron of the British fleet, detached to carry out a search, was making into the South Atlantic to lie across the customary shipping routes from Cape Horn. Or more likely any interception would wait off the western approaches to home waters where cover could be given against most Irish ports. He must be patient. But every nerve in his body was straining for the once so familiar sight of a British cruiser throwing up a bow wave as she sped through blue water to bring her great gun-batteries to bear . . .

It was next day before the sea and swell had subsided enough for the hands to go in amongst the cargo and sort out the mess. The Second Mate took charge, assisted by the carpenter. Halfhyde himself went down to take a look once the covers had been lifted from the hatches. Higgins was with him. Gaboon was on the bridge, which for the duration of Halfhyde's inspection had been left in the hands of the helmsman. Apart from the *Barry Island* there were no ships in sight to worry about, and needs must when the devil drove and a ship was short of officers.

Halfhyde, though expectant of a mess, was appalled at what he found. The whole cargo was lying up against the port bulkheads of the holds, higgledy-piggledy, and many of the cases had been split open. There were arms in profusion: revolvers, rifles – Lee Enfields as used by the British Army – Maxim guns even, grenades, box after box of ammunition. It would be manna even in the arsenal at Woolwich. There was a slop of water lapping around the confusion of cargo. As Halfhyde had said earlier, most of the consignment if not all would need individual cleaning and oiling; but Higgins was still unworried as to that aspect. The point was to get the armaments into Ireland. Halfhyde cast a cautious eye at the tumbled, broken cases: spread beneath him on the canted deck of the hold was any amount of weaponry if only he and Foster and the carpenter could get hold of it, but they wouldn't be allowed the chance. Higgins was already issuing his orders to cover that: Halfhyde's men were each to be marked by one of the suborned hands, who were to arm themselves from the cargo and shoot at sight if any attempt was made to seize a gun.

As the work was started, Halfhyde went back to the bridge. The *Barry Island* was lying off on his port quarter; reminded of cash shortages, he cursed to himself. The bills were mounting fast; Captain Thomas was losing day after day of his homeward voyage and his owners would want recompense for that. It was a hard fact of commercial sea life that no-one did anything for nothing, and owners always exacted no less than their pound of flesh. And largely starved their crews in the process ... Halfhyde was reminded of an old Yorkshire saying: *if thi does owt for nowt, do it for thissen.* Shipowners would probably have a parallel saying.

* * *

Perry walked the streets of Santiago with D'Arcy. The rest of the train journey had been diabolically uncomfortable but highly successful: D'Arcy had known exactly the moment to leave the train without being seen and all they had had to do, when the engine slowed outside the capital in the early morning, was to slide over the tailboard and drop down behind as the train chugged on. The unfenced track soon lay behind them and they were walking into the city's outskirts.

'I suppose,' D'Arcy said, 'this is where we part company, Mr Perry. Where do you propose to go?'

'The British Embassy,' Perry answered.

'To establish your innocence, to ask for protection?'

'That, yes.'

D'Arcy cocked an eye at him. 'You have a dubious sound. Is there anything else? But I'll not pry,' he added hastily. 'It's no business of mine. On the other hand, if you should want my help, it's there on offer for what it's worth.'

They walked on, coming into the heart of the capital. Perry was ruminating: D'Arcy had been a good friend and had proved his salvation already in getting him to Santiago. Besides, so far as Perry knew at any rate, he was untroubled by fears of the law and pursuit. By this time the hunt might be well and truly up. If so, then every moment held danger until he could reach the Embassy. It could well be a case of so near and yet so far. Although the main search would presumably be down in the south, around the country between Puerto Montt and Osorno, the wider aspects would certainly not be neglected, although, if an escape by train was assumed, Valparaiso would be considered a more likely final destination for a seaman than Santiago itself. But the police in Santiago would undoubtedly have been alerted as well; and it now seemed to Perry that there would be more than a chance that the British Embassy would be watched by the Chileans in case the fugitive should seek sanctuary there.

D'Arcy, on the other hand, could presumably approach the Embassy unhindered . . .

Perry reached a decision. He told D'Arcy the facts and indicated his orders from Halfhyde.

'Dear me,' D'Arcy said in concern. 'A pity you didn't tell me this earlier – but better late than never, and it's certainly not too late.'

'You'll help, then?'

'Of course I will – guns for the Irish rebels! I'm still a loyal Englishman, Mr Perry, and Her Majesty Queen Victoria is my sovereign and always will be. All you have to do is tell me how I can help.'

Perry did so: a visit to the Embassy, he said, on his behalf.

'H'm,' D'Arcy said. 'I doubt if much weight would be attached to a report from such as I, Mr Perry. It's more likely I'd be thought crazy, and treated as such.'

'I'm sure you could convince them,' Perry said.

'Perhaps, perhaps.' D'Arcy was obviously uneasy and reluctant. They walked on, with Perry casting glances all around as they came into the more crowded streets. Then D'Arcy came out with it: he and all British Embassies were best apart. 'A little trouble many years ago,' he said diffidently, 'but still upon the record, I fear. I am, you see, a bankrupt, Mr Perry. Whilst bankrupt I committed offences under the bankruptcy laws . . . seeking credit, you know. Paltry offences, but such as are, unfortunately, extraditable. I am sure you understand?'

'Yes,' Perry said somewhat ungraciously.

'I simply cannot return to England! We must find another way. I'm sure we can.'

'Suppose I'm apprehended by the police outside the Embassy?'

D'Arcy said, 'My dear fellow, now you've told me the facts, be sure I shall find some way of making them known if you're

133

unable to do so yourself. Meanwhile I suggest we take a discreet look at the Embassy.'

* * *

It was back-breaking work for the fo'c'sle crowd but at last the holds were restored to a proper stowage and the *Taronga Park* rode upright in the water. Right through the operations Higgins' men had maintained a close vigilance and, as Halfhyde had expected, there had been no opportunity of purloining a weapon of any sort. When the ship was back to her trim Captain Thomas brought the *Barry Island* close off the port beam and called across to make terms.

Halfhyde, having pondered the matter well by this time, had seen a solution. He answered that he would discuss no terms until his safe arrival in the United Kingdom, when he would accept the figure agreed by two independent assessors or imposed by the Admiralty court. After a good deal of argument, Captain Thomas agreed: he was unlikely to lose by it and Halfhyde was adamant, knowing that Thomas would be bound to accept his suggestion if he wished to be paid anything at all. A tow was once again passed and the *Barry Island* took up the strain; they proceeded through the now calm seas and under a warming sun, making around six knots. Halfhyde went to his charts and worked out an estimated time of arrival off the Fastnet: they were unlikely to make their landfall in less than twenty-one days. And a lot would depend on the weather ahead.

And what would Higgins do when the warships were sighted? They had to be ready for that. It was hard to assess just what the man's reaction would be to being taken; but Halfhyde doubted if there would be any tame submission. So did Victoria, when he talked to her later that day. 'He'll take a lot of us with him,' she said.

'I shall find a way round that.'

Cynically, she laughed. 'You're going to need a lot of luck,' she said. 'No guns – just nothing. What do you do?' He gave no answer; she went on, 'I'll tell you what you don't do. You don't worry about me. You just go right ahead and do what you have to. I've said before, I'm nothing. I mean that. But you know as well as I do, Higgins is going to make use of me against you.'

'He'll not get the chance,' Halfhyde said firmly, but the girl didn't believe him any more than he believed himself. It wouldn't take Higgins long to see that his game was up when the British warships hoisted the signal for the *Taronga Park* to heave to. Whether or not he worked out that there must have been a tip-off, he couldn't risk the possibility of a boarding-party examining the holds; even what he might take to be a random check on channel shipping would mean his immediate arrest and removal. He would go berserk. If he didn't, Gaboon would for a certainty.

* * *

Together Perry and D'Arcy had approached the Embassy, though not closely. Perry's fears mounted even though no uniformed police were to be seen. D'Arcy considered that strange in itself: one would, he said, have expected a formal guard to be provided by the Chileans. It could have been withdrawn for the very purpose of not scaring off the fugitive.

'It's a risk,' he said. 'The place *is* possibly under distant watch.'

'So what do you advise?'

'A strategic retreat. Give them a few days, long enough for them to become less watchful. I think you still have time in hand?'

Perry nodded: he had. He had worked out that he had spent a total of no less than eighteen days in his mostly delirious, semi-conscious state in the police cell at Puerto Montt; and altogether it was now twenty-five days since he had slid overboard from the *Taronga Park*, twenty-five days since Halfhyde had sailed on his voyage to the United Kingdom. Twenty-five days, assuming a reasonable mix of weather, should put the ship north of the equator but with almost half her run yet to do. Though he doubted if the Chilean police would become less watchful, time was on his side; but in the meantime he had to live and he had no money, nowhere to rest his head – nowhere to hide.

He put these points to D'Arcy.

D'Arcy waved them aside. 'The same applies to me, my dear fellow, apart from the need to hide from anyone but the Embassy, and I have made provision. I intended spending a while in the vicinity of Santiago. I know someone who can be trusted – and it is to her that we'll go, both of us. Will you place yourself in my hands, Mr Perry?'

Perry shrugged and said, 'I've been in them the last three days. Anyway, I reckon I've no option.'

'Gratefully expressed,' D'Arcy murmured. He turned about and led the way, moving back along the street, pushing through the crowds. After an immensely long walk they began to come clear of the city to the west. As they left the outskirts behind them, they came to dusty roads, little more than tracks, that led into hill slopes and an abundance of crops in a fertile-looking valley. Men and women were at work in the fields. D'Arcy, waving a hand towards them, said, 'There's always room for more people to work, if for a pittance, and that's what we shall do in return for food and shelter. You're game?'

Perry nodded. 'I've no wish to be a passenger.'

They trudged on. Perry's feet became blistered and sore; D'Arcy took it, literally, in his stride. Another few miles and then ahead of them they saw a long, low building half hidden by trees and set a hundred yards or so from the dusty track, with fields running into the distance behind and more men and women at work beneath a now lowering sun. D'Arcy led the way in through a gate and they approached the house, where an elderly woman was seated in a wickerwork chair on a shady verandah. Seeing the oncoming men she at first seemed startled; but then uttered a welcoming cry as she recognized D'Arcy. She rose to her feet and came forward, arms held wide as though about to embrace the unembraceable – both D'Arcy and Perry were by this time in a deplorable state of dust and sweat. She broke out into speech, voluble, a torrent of Spanish that was a long way beyond Perry's understanding, though D'Arcy seemed to have no difficulty.

He introduced Perry as a friend made on the road, and the elderly woman took his hand. She spoke to him in Spanish;

D'Arcy said, 'The *señora* has no English, Mr Perry, but she has a need of men to help in the harvest. We're very welcome.'

There was another conversation between D'Arcy and the *señora* and then the two Englishmen were taken to the kitchen quarters and given a meal. They ate and drank hungrily; and were then at once put to work in the fields behind the farmhouse. The task was to pick beans; and they picked until it was too dark to see. D'Arcy led the way to their quarters: a barn-like building with bunks in double tiers along the walls, now filling up with the men from the fields, men who dropped into the bunks fully dressed, weary from a day's work. D'Arcy and Perry talked for a while in low tones. D'Arcy, it seemed, had often worked, not too long at a time, for the *señora*, who had an abiding passion for him – according to himself. She was a widow, and ran the farm on her own, and she was intrigued by D'Arcy's history, realizing him to be a gentleman and having a strange veneration for English gentlemen as a species. 'A woman of good taste,' D'Arcy said gravely. 'I have to confess there are none like us . . .'

Perry drifted off to sleep. Next day they worked from dawn, right through the long day. And the next . . . On the third night Perry asked, more or less rhetorically, how he was ever going to make his report. Would there ever come a safe time? Would it not be better, perhaps, to risk re-arrest and then, once in custody, demand that someone from the Embassy should come to see him?

D'Arcy suggested that he might write a letter. This Perry obstinately refused to do. A letter might be disregarded – a letter from a person wanted by the Chilean police for murder. He must be there personally to convince: it was the only way way to carry out his orders. D'Arcy said there was no certainty that, if he were arrested, the Embassy staff would be allowed access to him.

It seemed to be an impasse.

That night Perry was woken by sounds coming from the bunk above him, D'Arcy's bunk. Sounds of distress . . . D'Arcy clambered down from his bunk and went outside. When he came back he said he had been sick. 'I have a headache,' he said. 'And it's very chilly.' Perry, by contrast, was suffering the close heat of the night. Next day D'Arcy seemed desperately tired, overcome by a strange lassitude, and that night he complained of tenderness of the stomach. In the morning he remained in his bunk; and Perry made the old woman understand that he was ill. Immediately she sent a man off on a horse to fetch the doctor. When the doctor came some hours later he diagnosed typhoid. D'Arcy, he said, was no longer young. He feared the worst.

He looked Perry up and down, closely. 'You are his friend?' he asked in English. 'You will nurse him for so long as he lasts, yes?'

Perry nodded. When the doctor had ridden away, Perry believed, in retrospect, that his searching look could have had more intent behind it than had been apparent at the time. An Englishman whose calling as a seaman was probably all too obvious, currently tramping the roads. There could by now have been posters up in Santiago and the adjacent districts.

Perhaps it was fortuitous that D'Arcy died late that afternoon. Perry would not have left him while he lived. But when he had drawn the coarse blanket over the lifeless face, he lost no time.

THIRTEEN

As the days passed the two ships, the tower and the towed, moved into flat seas beneath fair-weather skies. Higgins grew more and more confident as good progress was made towards the Fastnet. He had said nothing of his arrival plans to Halfhyde; but Halfhyde believed that Captain Thomas in the *Barry Island* would not wish to relinquish his tow until the *Taronga Park* was in the hands of the berthing pilot and the harbour tugs. Thus all unknowing Thomas would take the lethal cargo right to its Irish consignees.

Higgins did elaborate one morning, when Halfhyde had the bridge watch, on the use that was to be made of the arms cargo. It was not just to be those British military establishments in Ireland that he had spoken of once before; the battle, the battle for freedom as he called it, was to be taken to the British mainland. Small units of Irish patriots with well-concealed arms were to infiltrate via the ports – Fishguard, Liverpool, Stranraer and the Clyde – and go into hiding in the English cities. There would be isolated attacks on the military in Aldershot camp, in Colchester, Carlisle, Bodmin, Dorchester, Brighton, York – anywhere that held a military presence was likely to become the target for the *Taronga Park*'s cargo. London would not be exempt: the Tower, the barracks in Birdcage Walk, even Buckingham Palace itself would not be disregarded, the Queen's life not held sacrosanct.

'You'll never get away with it,' Halfhyde said.

Higgins smiled. 'I've already said, I don't propose to take part myself – I'm still merely the supplier. As to our fighting patriots, they're perfectly willing to lay down their lives. We have had many martyrs in Ireland, Halfhyde. There'll never be a shortage of volunteers, take my word for it!'

'And the actual value of all this?'

'In what way do you mean?'

'Don't you realize the sheer size of the British Army?'

'Certainly. But constant pinpricks, all causing loss of life – this will wear down morale and make the English realize that we're in earnest when we say we wish to run our own country, ourselves, in our own way. The English must be made to understand that we shall never give up the fight, and when we take the war on to their own soil on a much larger scale than Chester Castle . . . well, then they will see our determination.' Higgins' eyes were blazing with fervour; despite what he had said, he was not just the supplier of arms. There was dedication as well. In the last resort he, too, might be willing to lay down his life for the cause. That, however, remained to be seen: a determination had come to Halfhyde to put it to the test; and he had to be very sure that he got the first blow in. That Higgins would have to allow him to be on the bridge as they came up to the Fastnet was certain enough: a landsman would be flummoxed by any exchange of signals and by any need to work out the details of port entry with Captain Thomas. To a large extent Higgins would be in Halfhyde's hands – but the extent might not be large enough.

* * *

Across the seas in Chile, Perry's fears had been proved right: the police arrived at the farm just before nightfall. From cover up in the hills Perry saw them come in aboard a wagon drawn by two horses. He had got away just in time. Once again, with his confidante D'Arcy dead, he alone had the knowledge about the *Taronga Park*. Once again, it was all up to him.

He turned away and made deeper into the hills. The search, the drawing of the coverts as it were, would start at any moment. He was truly a hunted man now. His heart beat fast: currently he was heading away from the direction of Santiago and he saw no immediate prospect of going back the other way, saw, frankly, no prospect of getting inside the Embassy if ever he did reach the capital. If it hadn't been watched before – as he believed it had – then it certainly would be just as soon as the police reported back from the farm that the bird had flown.

What was he to do?

Stay hidden – if he could – until the local furore had died down, and then try to reach Santiago by a skirting movement, avoiding the farm, and risk an approach to the Embassy? There was, he believed, a telephone service, but he was unpractised on the telephone and could scarcely imagine himself conversing with some Spanish operator, trying to make himself understood on a totally unfamiliar instrument. Besides which, how did he find a telephone and how did he pay for its use? He had no money. In any case the Embassy might not be connected to the new-fangled telephone. Its use might not be considered consistent with diplomatic dignity and secrecy.

It was full dark now; Perry moved on, lost, stumbling about the rough country, intent only upon getting as far away as possible from any police presence; consideration of the future must be left for the time being.

After a while there was a bright moon to cast weird shadows and make him fancy danger where none existed. Looking down, he still saw the farm and its fields – he was much too close, but he found no sign of any search behind him. The police knew he was a seaman, unused to trekking about country districts, and they could be encircling the area, waiting for him to come out before he starved to death. Likely enough there was nothing edible growing in the hills; the moon showed him how barren they were. Barren and unfriendly, filled with pitfalls, things to trip over and fall full length so that flesh became bruised and grazed and himself more than ever of a vagabond. For the first time in his life, barring the recent weeks of his journey after leaving the *Taronga Park*, Perry was regretful that he was every inch a seaman. Such was of no help now. All his life had been spent either at sea or in seaports. Born and bred in Liverpool – son of a shipmaster, grandson of a bosun in the early ships of Lamport and Holt, pioneers of Liverpool's trade with the River Plate – Perry lived and breathed the sea. The shore constricted him; the country was a jungle.

When he believed he was far enough from the farm's vicinity he looked about for shelter. Finding it, he slept. He awoke with the sun, feeling his hunger sharply.

He had to decide what to do. He missed the friendly advice and companionship of D'Arcy. All around him was desolation, foothills, forests. And his captain was relying implicitly upon him, fully confident, surely, that by now his report had already been telegraphed to London. To let him down, to let the ship down, was detestable and craven.

Perry made up his mind: he would brazen it out and head directly for the Embassy. Often enough the simple and direct approach was the best. He might be lucky and get a sympathetic hearing from the police when they arrested him. He could see no other way now.

* * *

When it was too late, Perry realized he had made a mistake: he should have risked it and gone back to the farm. It was unlikely any police guard had been left on the chance the fugitive might come back. The old woman had been friendly and D'Arcy had trusted her. She might have got a message to the Embassy . . . but it was no good thinking now of what might have been. He had gone to far to return.

He trudged on. He had chosen a long way precisely so as to avoid having to go near the farm and its environs. His route was taking him north for a while, then he would turn eastward and drop down on Santiago.

He passed the odd peasant.

'*Buenos dias* . . .' Polite greetings were exchanged and that was all; he remained unremarked. The journey took all that day and most of the succeeding night. It was in the early hours of the following morning when he came again into Santiago's outskirts, a different approach from the one he'd made with D'Arcy. He was soon lost and by now he was desperately hungry even though after coming down from the hills he had found a little wild fruit and had managed to drink from a stream. He knew he'd been lucky to get this far. From now on, he would need a lot more luck. In seamen's terms, he was standing into danger. And he needed sleep, rest for feet that felt like balls of fire.

Moving on he found a church. He went in; a church offered sanctuary. There was a smell of incense and candles burned on a side altar. It was very peaceful. Perry sat in a pew, slumped to his knees, fell sideways, and slept. Soon a priest came down the aisle, quietly, almost ghost-like in the candle flames. He looked down at the sleeping man, smiled, made the sign of the Cross, and went back whence he had come. After sleeping for four hours, Perry woke to the sound of an organ softly played. He sat up, then got on his knees and offered a prayer that he might reach the Embassy. Leaving the church and the quietness, he went out into a street already beginning to bustle with early business.

Taking a risk, he asked the way to the British Embassy. Given general directions to the capital's more elegant quarter, he went on. After another long walk he found himself in surroundings made familiar by his visit with D'Arcy; and soon he was able to recognize the Embassy building.

Resolutely, he walked towards it, conscious of his travel-stained appearance. As he neared the gates, he became aware of persons closing in: one ahead, one behind. The one ahead called out to him in Spanish, presumably an order to stop. When he didn't do so, the man pulled out a revolver.

Perry broke into a run towards the gate. There was a man there, obviously one of the Embassy staff, looking startled. Perry was not far from the gate when the armed man opened fire. He missed; a bullet sped past Perry's head and ricocheted off the gate.

He ran on desperately, for his life. He had reached the gate's sanctuary when he was hit by three bullets. One took him a glancing blow on the side of the head and everything went blank. The force of impact from the other two bullets sent his body flying through the gateway and Embassy staff began running out from the building.

* * *

143

He came round for a brief period after he had been carried into the Embassy. Faces were peering down at him, faces of authority. He heard one of the men say that the Chilean police had stated that he was the wanted man. There was talk of Osorno, and the murder charge. Perry pushed his tongue through dry lips and tried to speak. Everything was going round in circles and he felt immense pain somewhere, while other parts seemed numb. His back, his hip . . . after a while his voice came, with difficulty.

'A message,' he said in no more than a whisper. 'A message . . . for London.'

That was all he could manage. He was dimly aware of much concern in the faces bending over him and then unconsciousness came back.

Above him the British Minister – Chile was not in fact accorded an ambassador – straightened and looked perplexed. 'A message,' he said wonderingly. 'This is a devilish problem, I must say! The Chileans have their rights but I'll want to know a lot more before I hand him over. His name . . . Perry, is it?'

'Yes, Minister,' the First Secretary said. 'That is, if he's the Osorno one.'

'And the ship?'

'The *Taronga Park*, Sydney for Queenstown.'

'Yes . . . I wonder what the devil that message is.' The Minister blew out his cheeks. 'We must assume it's of some importance, if only in the man's mind. Unless it was just a ploy to get our help. Have you sent for a doctor, Matthews?'

The First Secretary nodded. As they waited, in more than a little indecision, the doctor was brought in by a servant. He made a quick examination. There was, he said, a bullet in the right hip, another more importantly lodged in the intestine, right against the spine, he believed. He suspected paralysis; and the man had already lost a lot of blood. His recovery was doubtful; but he must be removed to hospital without delay, for the removal of the bullets.

The Minister made a rapid decision, thinking of that message. 'He'll be treated here,' he said. 'He's not leaving Embassy ground. Nurses, operating equipment. Make all the arrangements, Matthews, and quickly.'

'Sir, the Chilean—'

'I'll deal with the Chileans myself. You'd better contact the President's office and ask for an audience on a matter of great importance concerning a British subject shot at inside the Embassy gates by his damn policemen . . .'

Within the next few minutes Perry was lifted on to a stretcher and carried up a flight of stairs to a bedroom that was already being turned into a makeshift operating theatre. Soon after he had been laid on the bed, still with the stretcher beneath his body, a table was manhandled up the stairs and set up ready for the doctor, who had not been allowed to leave the Embassy in the meantime. After some delay while telephone calls were exchanged with the President, in the course of which the Minister indicated tartly that there had been an intrusion into British sovereign territory and that his government in London would be informed, nurses arrived together with another doctor and a bag of instruments. In the event Perry came through the primitively conducted operation but remained unconscious for a suspiciously long time afterwards. The doctor was baffled: the man, he said, could undoubtedly have struck his head when falling after being shot, but there was no apparent sign of injury. Heads, however, were funny things and it was somewhat beyond his ability to cope with what went on inside the human brain.

Perry remained unconscious and breathing heavily as many days passed. He had still said nothing beyond that first indication of a message. In the interval the Minister had been given a report on the *Taronga Park*. Checks had been made by cable with Sydney. The ship was carrying a cargo of cased machine parts for Ireland. Her master was one St Vincent Halfhyde; little was known either of him or of the First Mate, Perry, other than that there were no black marks against him. The shipper of the cargo was one Porteous Higgins, an Irishman resident in Sydney. Higgins, it seemed, was no longer in Sydney and his whereabouts were unknown. There was nothing in the report to cast doubts on Higgins' character and the Embassy certainly had no knowledge of him.

'I'm not entirely satisfied,' the Minister said to his First Secretary. 'The fellow may well be a murderer – but I'm still not handing him over. Not yet. I want some more information from him first . . . I don't see why he came to the Embassy if he was guilty. He must have known we'd have to hand him over eventually.'

* * *

That night, without ever regaining consciousness, Perry died. The news was taken at once to the Minister, who shrugged. The death had relieved him of further worry; there was nothing more he could be called upon to do, no more decisions, and even the Chilean authorities would presumably be satisfied that the man, if he was a murderer, had paid the penalty. The case could proceed no further now, at all events. Burial would be arranged and both Sydney and London would be informed so that any next-of-kin could be told.

Many days later, away across the Pacific in Sydney, Mr William Sturt, director of the Australian Joint Stock Bank, lay mostly sleepless in his bed. He had received word that there was a query from Santiago in Chile in regard to the steamship *Taronga Park*, in whose master Sturt was well known to have taken an interest, whose finance he had arranged for the purchase of the ship. Sturt was suffering pangs of conscience: Halfhyde had, after all, confided in him as to the true nature of his cargo. At that time he had failed to offer practical help; now Halfhyde's First Mate had, it seemed, been charged with murder . . . there were no details about that. Sturt was left to use his imagination. How had Perry come to be left ashore in Chile? Was there any connection between Perry's alleged act of murder and Halfhyde's cargo?

Could he, William Sturt, be in any way drawn in – perhaps as an accessory since he had been given the knowledge of the arms cargo? Halfhyde might have mentioned that to someone – Perry, Higgins?

Word had filtered through to him from certain private sources that Porteous Higgins had boarded the *Taronga Park*. If so, he was now well away from Sydney. Sturt pondered. There

146

was danger to himself if he now intervened, danger from Porteous Higgins, but if Higgins really was aboard the ship . . . two birds with one stone?

And then that matter of conscience. In truth he had been disturbed for a long time now; there would be blood on his hands even though there was a chance that if Halfhyde hadn't passed it on, no-one need ever know – except for Halfhyde himself. But what was Perry doing in the Santiago Embassy, for God's sake? *Had* something come out, something the Embassy was not releasing?

Sturt sweated, moving restlessly in his bed. When at last he fell into an uneasy sleep he was the prey to terrible nightmares. Blood was welling from the holds of the *Taronga Park*, pouring out to drown him while Porteous Higgins looked on, laughing. Porteous Higgins vanished and his place was taken by rebel Irish peasants with tails and pitchforks emerging from the fires of hell. Then he was in a courtroom, faced by a judge about to have the black cap placed on his head while he mouthed words about treason and a terrible responsibility for facilitating murder and the destruction of the Queen's property in Ireland.

The nightmares faded with the morning light and brought sanity. Part of the sanity was a knowledge that he must do something to clear his yardarm. After many days of dither Sturt began to compose a cable to the British Minister in Santiago de Chile. Certain matters, that cable said, had come to his attention . . . certain irregularities. He had no precise knowledge of chicanery, but the *Taronga Park* might be worth investigating upon arrival in Queenstown. He made no specific mention of an arms cargo.

FOURTEEN

The approach to home waters was made in the early morning of what promised to be a fine day, good towing weather for a crippled ship to enter port. Halfhyde picked up the Fastnet light almost at the extremity of its eighteen-mile range.

'That's it,' he said to Higgins. 'The Fastnet.'

'How far now?' Higgins demanded.

'I'm sure you've looked at the chart.'

Higgins turned on him. 'I asked, how far now?'

Halfhyde shrugged. 'From here, about twenty-two miles to Cape Clear, on an east-nor'-easterly course. From Cape Clear to the entrance to Cork harbour, sixty miles.'

'So we'll be off the entrance in about – what?'

'Fourteen to fifteen hours, possibly a little more. We're not making much speed.'

Higgins turned his back again and stared out ahead. There was scarcely any wind, just enough for the freshness of the early morning to be appreciated. Gradually the sky lightened and soon, distantly, the Irish coastline could be seen, as yet not much more than a blur on the horizon.

At 3.45 Foster came up the bridge to relieve the Captain; Halfhyde handed over the watch and went below. The girl was in his cabin, sound asleep. He hadn't intended waking her; but she stirred and opened her eyes. He gave her a report: not far to go and no British ships in the vicinity.

She said, 'Oh, bloody hell.'

'I'm not worried. I expect them to be held further in, off the entrance. Or they may not show even then.' Halfhyde believed

148

the Admiralty might even decide to allow the *Taronga Park* into the port and send off a boarding-party from the Naval base at Haulbowline to cook Higgins' goose for him. Once inside, there would be a strong Naval presence and Higgins would be helpless. He told Victoria this.

'Won't he smell something out before going in?' she asked.

'There's no reason why he should. He's never been worried about Perry going over the side. There's been no other contact.'

'No,' she said, frowning. 'That's true enough. I just thought . . . well, it's going to look a little too easy for him, isn't it?'

He smiled down at her as he pulled his clothing off. 'I say again, there's no reason why it should. Plenty of people in fact get away with smuggling – arms, spirits, anything. Higgins isn't the only man who's ever supplied guns to the Irish!'

'No customs check?'

'Possibly not – when there's a contraband aboard and the arrival's been prepared in advance. Money works wonders – you should know that from your knowledge of Higgins—'

'Sure,' she said. 'I do.' She still seemed uneasy. 'Just don't get too confident, that's all. Your Mr Perry, he may never have got through for all you know. Higgins still has the whip hand till the Navy comes aboard. I've seen him get out of tight corners before now.'

'He won't get out of this one,' Halfhyde said with assurance. Now that the Irish coast was coming up, all his doubts, all his fears other than for the girl herself, had vanished. Higgins had shot his bolt and although he might turn at bay like a tiger when the end came, he was doomed in the upshot to spend long years in a British gaol with his cargo confiscated. Halfhyde was convinced that nothing could go wrong now. His own part in this was henceforward confined to the protection of his ship and those of his crew who had remained loyal to him throughout the long voyage . . .

Victoria was studying his face, and smiling. She said, 'You've been a long while gone. Up on the bridge, I mean. Reckon you just want sleep and nothing else, now?'

The invitation, the hope, was obvious. He smiled back at her, feeling happy, relaxed. 'I'll sleep, but all in good time,' he said.

He was about to take her in his arms when the facts of the voyage returned with sudden harshness. There was a sound in the doorway behind him and he swung round, noting as he did so the fear that had come to the girl's eyes.

Gaboon stood there with a revolver aimed at him. There was a salacious leer on Gaboon's face. The root of his tongue, as the thick lips parted, swelled with an influx of blood. With his free arm he indicated the girl, then jerked the hand backwards over his shoulder, through the open door. Halfhyde took a pace forward, his eyes hard. Sudden fury overcame him and he disregarded the revolver. Gaboon backed away from him but behind the hairy figure two more men moved into view, two of the fo'c'sle hands, each of them carrying a revolver. Behind again was another man, one of the black gang from the silent stokehold, carrying a marline-spike. From behind Halfhyde the girl spoke. She said, 'It's all right, I'll go. I told you, you're not to think about me.'

She got out of bed, picked up a dressing-gown and pushed past him, and they took her away, down the ladder to the well-deck and into the after accommodation. The door from the well-deck was banged shut behind her. Higgins was making his final dispositions already.

* * *

The cable from Sydney was not brought immediately to the attention of the Minister. It had reached the Embassy while he was at luncheon, entertaining some Chilean military and naval officers, high-ranking personages, and *prima facie* the cable did not appear to have the urgency to warrant an intrusion upon Ministerial hospitality. The First Secretary brought it to him at a little after four o'clock that afternoon.

'What do you think, Matthews?' the Minister asked.

'I see a connection with the man Perry, Minister—'

'Ah, yes. The *Taronga Park* – and the message he was anxious about. Well, well. A warning – he was trying to pass a warning, poor fellow! If only he'd lived . . .' The Minister dabbed at his cheeks with a linen handkerchief; the day was a hot one and he'd taken a large luncheon. 'Nothing we can do, of course.

You'd better pass it to London, I suppose. We can't disregard it, but it's going to lead to a number of questions that I'll not be able to answer . . .'

Within an hour, another cable was encoded and passed to the Foreign Office in London. This cable included the Minister's comments on Perry, First Mate of the suspect ship. It was not given any special priority and it was not until the following morning that it was brought to the attention of a Senior Clerk, next in the Foreign Office heirarchy to the Permanent Under-Secretary. The Senior Clerk did not find it necessary to trouble his superior; the Minister in Santiago was, of course, perfectly correct to pass the information to the Foreign Office, but the affair was better dealt with by the Board of Trade, who could pass it for action to the Board of Customs. When, eventually, word reached the Board of Customs there was no indication whatever that there might even be bloodshed, that in a sense piracy had taken place – insofar as the *Taronga Park*'s master was no longer in command – and it never occurred to anyone that the Admiralty should be asked for boarding assistance or the provision of a warship. But Customs and Excise at Queenstown were informed by yet another cable carrying instructions that the *Taronga Park*'s holds were to be opened up and the cargo closely examined. It was left to the senior officer of customs at the port to decide whether or not to ask for Naval assistance from Haulbowline Island.

At Queenstown this message was opened by the second-in-command of the customs station. There was no need, he decided, to bother his senior; he could board the *Taronga Park* himself. His name was Seamus McBride. He was alone in his office; he struck a match and watched the message form curl in his fingers. When the day's work was finished he walked along to a bar behind a grocer's shop. He drank a pint of Guinness, slowly. He had almost finished it when a small, dark-eyed man with a long upper lip and a swarthy complexion came into the bar. Very briefly, their eyes met. Then McBride drank the remains of his Guinness and went out. Some ten minutes later he was passed in the street by the small man, whom he followed out of the town, keeping his distance. Already the *Taronga Park* had been reported inward bound and under tow. The towing vessel had signalled an engine-room breakdown. Proceeding at slow speed, she was expected to enter Cork harbour that evening at seven o'clock to be berthed by the harbour tugs.

There was time in hand yet.

* * *

As evening drew on and the final act loomed, the tension had come back to the ship. Higgins paced the bridge, keeping a sharp watch all around as the entry to the port came up and the harbour tugs nosed busily out beneath smoke-belching funnels to take over the tow from the *Barry Island*. Halfhyde was worried by the total absence of British ships in the approaches but not yet too despondent: his thoughts about a boarding-party from Haulbowline were no doubt correct after all. The *Taronga Park* was but one small ship, perhaps not considered of enough importance to warrant sudden redispositions of the British fleet. Haulbowline could deal well enough with arms smuggling.

Fervently, he hoped so. If anything should have gone wrong, if Perry had fallen by the wayside, then not only would the Irish patriots get their weapons but he and the girl and the loyal men such as Foster were scarcely likely to come out alive.

Yet succour would come; it had to. Perry would never have failed him. The message would most surely have been passed to someone in Chile.

Captain Evan Thomas was shouting across to him, something about the tugs. Halfhyde took up his megaphone and called back.

'The tugs'll take over, Captain, but be assured you'll get your full salvage. You have my word.' He paused. 'If you wish, you can follow me in and obtain my signature.' And to hell with Porteous Higgins, he thought savagely; but Higgins would have none of that.

He said, 'Tell Thomas he's not wanted in the port, Halfhyde, or you'll suffer, and so will the girl.'

There was no need for that. Thomas shouted back, 'I shall if

152

necessary obtain the witness of the tugmasters, Captain, do not worry. As for me, I must take my ship on to Barry dock . . . in my owner's interests, you see.'

Somewhat forlornly, Halfhyde gave Thomas a wave. 'I understand. Thank you a thousand times for your long assistance, Captain.'

'It is all right, you are welcome.'

Aboard the *Barry Island* hands moved aft to cast off the tow-line, and the *Taronga Park* drifted free until the harbour tugs nosed in, one passing a line for'ard to take the strain while the other manoeuvred into position on the starboard quarter to push her fendered stem against the plating. The pilot jumped from his boat on to the jacob's ladder slung out on the port side amidships, and climbed to the bridge. He took off his bowler hat to Halfhyde.

'A long voyage, Captain.' He glanced at Higgins with an interrogative look, caught by Higgins himself.

'A privileged passenger,' Higgins said shortly.

Halfhyde was becoming more alarmed now; surely, if the Naval authorities at Haulbowline had been alerted and there was to be a full customs search, then the pilot would have been warned and would have reacted differently, with a cautious and possibly nervous reserve? But perhaps not; pilots would have seen many incidents during their careers and this was just one more day's work that could hold little danger once the hatches were opened up.

As the pilot, using his whistle, passed his orders to the tugs, the *Taronga Park* moved slowly inwards. By now the *Barry Island* had hauled away on her course for the Bristol Channel, her engine moving ahead fast, freed of the tow, with thick black smoke pouring from her funnel as her furnaces were banked up. The arms of the land, a suddenly hostile land, reached out to enfold the vessel home from distant seas. Almost all the crew were on deck, acting under Higgins' orders now. A moment later Halfhyde saw the customs launch coming off, with two officers standing in the sternsheets.

This is it, he thought. His body stiffened involuntarily for the encounter: his mind was partly on his ship, partly on the girl being held below by Gaboon. Higgins had been explicit: if anything went wrong by any act of Halfhyde's or Foster's, the girl would die. Gaboon would carry out his orders; Gaboon would never back-track – he wouldn't dare to and wouldn't want to. He and Higgins might swing, but the threat stood and Halfhyde fully believed it. Higgins had to have a positive sanction, and this was it.

Once again the jacob's ladder was used; the customs officers came aboard, were taken to the Captain's cabin by a deckhand. The customs didn't interfere with pilotage; their business would come once the ship was berthed alongside. When the lines had been secured and the tugs were chuffing away smokily across the harbour Halfhyde, accompanied by Higgins, went below to his cabin. Two deckhands loafed about the master's desk outside the ports; their casual air was unconvincing. In the cabin, the customs officers got down to their work briskly, asking for the cargo manifest and the bills of lading. Halfhyde produced them and waited expectantly while they were gone through. He offered whisky; the customs men accepted and Butcher brought glasses and a bottle. Halfhyde watched Porteous Higgins; it was becoming a close thing but the man seemed at ease, utterly unconcerned, and Halfhyde's anxieties increased. When the check of the documents was finished, the senior customs man, McBride, looked up at Halfhyde.

'Everything's in order, Captain. You've had no problems, I take it?'

No problems, everything in order . . . Halfhyde felt the prickle of real danger. Clearly, no message had come through from Santiago. He recalled the gist of what he'd said earlier to the girl, that many men had successfully smuggled guns into Ireland – when the customs had been bribed, prepared in advance. Halfhyde felt the sweat break out. It was Porteous Higgins who answered McBride's question: there had been no problems.

Halfhyde asked hoarsely, 'Do you not propose to examine the cargo, Mr McBride?'

'No, no. That'll not be necessary at all. You're free to start unloading whenever you wish, Captain.' McBride pulled a turnip-shaped watch from his waistcoat pocket. 'I must be away to the shore. Thank you for the whisky, Captain.' He went with his accomplice to the cabin door; Halfhyde caught the brief look that passed between him and Porteous Higgins. As the officials were heard clattering down the ladder to the fore well-deck and the shore gangway, Higgins gave Halfhyde a look of triumph. Halfhyde was stymied and knew it – they both knew it. Halfhyde could have come out with anything to the customs and no notice would have been taken. Higgins was the paymaster. And what to do now? Start a fight that might be heard ashore, so that Haulbowline could be alerted to trouble aboard the ship? But do that, and what happened to the helpless girl in Gaboon's wicked hands? In any case it was too late now: Higgins was armed and ready and the man from the black gang had moved in behind with his marline-spike. One move, one shout that in all probability would be heard only by the retreating customs men, and Halfhyde would have his skull stove in. Dead, he could never hit back at Porteous Higgins . . .

Higgins said, smirking, 'We'll waste no time now.'

The unloading was started within the next ten minutes under the light of a masthead group, a metal-backed cluster of electric light bulbs hoisted to the port fore yardarm. As the cases were brought on the whip of the derrick to the well-deck, horse-drawn transport rumbled out of the darkness on to the quay and pulled up alongside ready to take the slings. Men came aboard to talk to Higgins, men with thick Irish accents, clandestine men with an air of anger about them as they set foot aboard an English ship. Quickly they got on with the job, taking over the cargo as it came up in the slings to be hoisted over the side from the well-decks fore and aft. One by one the horse-drawn wagons were loaded and one by one they were driven away from the harbour. While this was going on Higgins set to work paying off the disaffected fo'c'sle hands, his own mob, a liberal bonus in each fistful of golden sovereigns which he had brought out from his gear. He gave a warning about loose tongues. He would take his revenge on any man who uttered. His arm, he said, was a long one; the best they could do was to find a ship and sign for a foreign voyage – back if they wished for their homes in Sydney, the *Taronga Park*'s home port until she had been bought by Halfhyde. But nowhere would they be free of Porteous Higgins and nor would their families, if ever they opened their mouths. And accessories were wise to keep silent for their own sakes.

There was something different in store for the few hands who had remained loyal: with Halfhyde and Foster and the girl, they would leave the ship with Higgins and Gaboon. And as the last loaded wagon was pulled away from the docks, they went with it, surrounded by grim-faced Irishmen.

* * *

Shortly before the *Taronga Park* had cast off the *Barry Island*'s tow the message from Santiago, passed by the Foreign Office to the Board of Trade and thence to customs, was by sheer chance brought to the attention of an official more highly placed than the one who had passed it on disinterestedly to the Board of Customs. This official pondered over it, frowning. A cargo, unspecified in the message, for Ireland, a cargo that was being called into question.

There could be more in this than met the eye.

Someone in Australia had taken the trouble to cable word through to Santiago, evidently as the result of some query from the British Minister in that city. The official looked up at the underling who had drawn his eye to the matter. He said, 'The Admiralty should be informed, I fancy. A precautionary measure, that's all.'

His order was quickly carried out. But in the Admiralty the message met further delay; the hour was late by this time and the matter was not dealt with until the following morning, when a desk-bound Captain in Her Majesty's fleet read urgency into it at last. That new-fangled instrument, the telephone, was brought into use. There was much cranking of handles and along the line to Ireland many exchanges answered and passed on the call. It was not a fast process; but when the message reached the Captain-in-Charge at Haulbowline Island in Cork Harbour no more time was lost.

The bosun's calls began shrilling out over the Naval establishment and a guard was quickly mustered under a Sub-Lieutenant and a gunner's mate. But when this party, aboard a steam pinnace, came alongside the quay and marched to the *Taronga Park*'s gangway, Halfhyde and the rest were many miles inland and the ship's holds were empty and the decks deserted.

When later the Sub-Lieutenant made contact with the customs, he was assured by Seamus McBride that the cargo had been totally innocuous: cased machine parts, McBride said, as per cargo manifest. He was unable to account for the fact that the whole crew had left the ship. He suggested the drink; it had been a long voyage, made worse by the need for a slow passage under tow.

* * *

They had been driven through the night as fast as whipped-up horses could manage, lying with bound wrists and ankles in the back of the wagon under a heavy tarpaulin, with Higgins and Gaboon on the box beside the driver. In the early hours they had gone to ground in County Kerry, on the fringe of the Boggeragh Mountains. It was wet, with a chill wind; the land was wild and empty, eerie with the howl of the wind. Hidden by trees as they pulled off a narrow, rutted track they found the wagons that had left Queenstown before them. They were drawn up into a kind of laager with four of the Irishmen mounting a guard while the rest slept. They remained there for the rest of the night and into the morning; around noon three men and two women arrived as if from nowhere, bringing hampers of food with them, and a meal was taken. The prisoners were given enough to keep them going. While, still bound, they were fed, Halfhyde picked up snatches of talk; it seemed that the arms consignment was expected by a detachment of the patriots in the mountains of Connemara in County Galway, still some way to the north, in the lonely province of Connacht. The convoy remained under cover until dark; and when once again it got on the move with Higgins and Gaboon, the only prisoner to go with it was the girl. Halfhyde and the rest, now with their ankles free but their hands still tied, were led away through the trees by the men and women who had come with the food.

With guns in their backs they were marched for some distance before being halted on the fringe of flat ground that could be seen stretching interminably ahead as the moon stole through a break in heavy cloud. The ground looked lifeless, with nothing growing except for some scrubby, coarse grass; but in places there seemed to be a heaving, sucking motion.

FIFTEEN

Captain Warrender of the Royal Navy, Captain-in-Charge at
Haulbowline, was studying papers brought from the *Taronga
Park*, papers from the master's cabin.

'St Vincent Halfhyde,' he said thoughtfully to his First
Lieutenant. 'The name's familiar. I wonder . . . bring me the
Navy List, if you please.'

The Navy List was brought. Warrender flipped through the
pages. He found Halfhyde's name among the retired officers of
the fleet. 'Thought so,' he said. 'It's coming back to me. St
Vincent Halfhyde . . . married Admiral Willard's daughter –
what was her name – Miss Mildred. Then left the service.
Dammit – a retired officer, an admiral's son-in-law – his cargo
must have been in order! In any case we have the word of the
customs fellow, McBride – he's always been perfectly trustworthy.'

'So far as we know, sir.'

Warrender looked up sharply. 'Are you suggesting something, First Lieutenant?'

'Only that it's unusual to find a ship totally deserted, sir.'

'Yes . . . I agree about that, of course. And the Admiralty
seems concerned.' Warrender frowned, running over his First
Lieutenant's full report in his mind. The *Taronga Park* had been
found shipshape enough, though the damage in the engine-
room had carried the hallmarks of a deliberate act intended to
impede the ship's progress – an act of sabotage. There had been
evidence of a shifted cargo, due no doubt to bad weather on
passage. Otherwise there was nothing to give any clue as to

159

what the cargo might genuinely have been, assuming the Admiralty's anxieties to be well founded. But there was that overriding consideration of an apparently abandoned ship. No former Naval officer would be so in dereliction of his duty as to leave his command without even a watchman aboard and Captain Warrender, a slow man to make up his mind, a cautious officer at all times, knew he had to act on that contributory evidence alone.

He said, 'We'll have to inform the constabulary, and the officer commanding the military garrison.'

'Aye, aye, sir. I'll see to it at once.'

Too much time had been wasted already. When informed, the Superintendent of the Royal Irish Constabulary made the point forcefully. He would act immediately. For a start, he said, the environs of the port would be toothcombed for any member of the *Taronga Park*'s crew who might be found drink-laden in the many bars. And the customs would be interviewed by himself personally.

* * *

'Keep moving,' the man behind Halfhyde said. He prodded with his revolver. Halfhyde walked on behind the woman acting as a guide through what was obviously one of Ireland's larger bogs. The pathway, the firm strip of ground, was apparently fairly wide but Halfhyde knew that a false step could be fatal. Strict single file was being maintained and each of the prisoners – Halfhyde, Foster, Thompson the carpenter, steward Butcher, the two seamen O'Dowd and Byers – had a gun in his back. They walked for a long way, and mostly in silence. The moon remained bright, silvering the dreary landscape with a ghostly light. Occasionally a bird cried out eerily. To Halfhyde and the others, accustomed to the wide open spaces of the sea, it was a nightmare journey. It was like thick fog at sea; no-one could be certain of what might lie ahead or on either side. But at last it ended when the woman turned round and said, 'We're through, Mr O'Reilly.'

'The Lord be praised for that,' one of the men said from the rear of the line. The single file was broken up, and the men and women with the guns moved to bunch the prisoners and surround them. There were trees ahead, and in the midst of them a small white-washed cottage with a roof of thatch, a tiny cabin marooned in the bog and consisting, as Halfhyde saw when he ducked under the low doorway, of a single room with a fireplace in which a turf fire burned to give some warmth and light enough to see. With the rest of his men he was herded towards the other end of the room, away from the fire.

The man addressed as O'Reilly came forward with his revolver pointed. 'Here you stay,' he said. ' 'Tis a lonely place and one from which you'll not get away unless you wish to be suffocated in the bog. But just to make sure, you'll have your ankles tied again.'

'What's the idea?' Halfhyde asked. 'The bog's a handy enough disposal place, I'd have thought—'

'You're wanted yet,' O'Reilly said.

'What for?'

There was a laugh. 'Not by Higgins. He's done with you. By us! Have you never heard of hostages?'

Halfhyde stared through the gloom. At the other end of the cabin someone was stirring up the turf fire, and more red light came, silhouetting the Irish patriots and giving them the aspect of devils. 'Hostages against what – or whom?'

The man laughed again, a nasty sound. 'Never mind that,' he said. ' 'Tis our business. It may be you'll not be needed in the end. And once you're not needed, the bog'll still be there.'

* * *

Higgins' wagon train had split up by the time Higgins himself had reached Connemara, well to the north of Halfhyde's current situation. Three days after leaving Queenstown, Galway City was skirted under cover of darkness as Higgins headed towards Tuam, while the loaded wagons made their way independently to their pre-arranged destinations in the fastnesses of Connemara where they would remain hidden until the day for the rising came. To hide would be far from difficult; Connemara, wild and lonely, mountainous, sea-girt on its western side, with far-stretching bogs lying as traps between sea and mountains, was the ideal place for the wherewithal of insurrection, ambush and murder. Connemara, all of Connacht in fact, was sparsely populated; the roads were lonely and once a man had gone north of Galway City he would find few habitations except in towns such as Tuam or Gort. Of those who did live in the desolate country areas most had illicit stills and such, and were no lovers of the law. Here in Ireland's west the forces of law and order walked warily; any man's hand could be against them and over the years there had been many unexplained disappearances, many constables, soldiers and excisemen shot in ambushes and the killers never found. In Connemara, no man knew anything when questioned. The peasant inhabitants, bog Irishmen, few of whom spoke English with any facility, formed a tight clan against outsiders and more so against the police.

Porteous Higgins felt the sheer loneliness and sensed the brooding quality of the district. With Gaboon and the girl he made the last few miles of the journey on foot, guided by a man provided from the wagon train. His personal hiding place lay in the wildness of the country some miles south of Tuam – the cottage of a man named Casey, where Higgins was to await payment for his arms consignment.

Weary by now, he was relieved when the cottage came into view in the dawn's light. It was a small place, white-washed walls beneath a thatched roof, with the Connemara Mountains behind. Casey came out to meet his visitors: Casey was tall and dark, a saturnine Irishman with a long, thin face. He ushered the three inside. Victoria was told off to heat a saucepan of water over the turf fire, in preparation for washing. Casey had no wife; by the fire sat an old woman, Casey's mother as it turned out, a seamed and wizened crone who did nothing, Casey said, but nod and chew toothless gums and offer words of criticism. Under her tongue, though the words couldn't be understood, Victoria prepared the hot water, moving almost as an automaton, utterly dispirited by now. Such a place . . . there would be no chance of escape even if she could elude Gaboon.

Higgins asked about the payment.

Casey said, 'The man'll be here soon. He'll be doing the

paying.'

'What man?'

'We don't speak his name,' Casey said. 'Just – the man.'

* * *

In the cabin by the bog, they had been left alone. Their ankles were tied again and they had been roughly gagged. At the other end of the room the fire had died down; the day grew cold; they heard the whine of the wind, gusting and tugging at the thatch. That thatch was in poor condition; one corner was bare, daylight and rain came through. Halfhyde rolled his body along the floor, bringing his face into contact with all manner of filth, until he lay out of the rain's path.

Nearer the remains of the fire, and some warmth.

He rolled further.

There was still a flicker of life; the stone surround and the floor of the fireplace itself gave out a fair heat and would continue to do so for a while. Foster rolled across behind Halfhyde, followed by the others.

Halfhyde stared at the turf fire. By now it was largely white ash and very powdery, but one segment, oblong-shaped, was smouldering redly beneath. If only he could get at it. He manoeuvred his bound body closer to the fire and reached out his knees. He managed to contact the smouldering segment. He cursed behind the gag: he had merely sent it further towards the back of the fireplace. He tried again: lifting his knees, he got them over the turf and jerked them towards his body and the turf turned over, smouldering side uppermost. Gritting his teeth, he rolled over until his tied wrists were closer to the turf segment. Forcing his body backwards, he extended his wrists as far as he could, pushing back until he felt the searing pain as his wrists came down on the last of the fire. He felt his flesh burn, smelled burning cloth as his jacket caught the ember.

* * *

In the streets of Queenstown no drunken seamen were picked up. None of the bar proprietors, mostly the grocers, had any knowledge of the crew of the *Taronga Park*. There had been no

163

spree. The clue came in the end from the railway station. A number of men, obviously seamen, had taken the train the night before to Cork City; enquiries in Cork City brought the information that a similar number of seamen from Queenstown had bought tickets for Dublin. Dublin was contacted by the telephone, but it was assumed that the men had boarded the ferry for Liverpool or Holyhead and would by now have dispersed in England. They might be apprehended whilst looking for berths aboard the outward-bounders and the police in Liverpool and North Wales were asked to assist.

Meanwhile the Irish police and the army were already starting a widespread search for the *Taronga Park*'s vanished cargo and a number of persons were being questioned.

No-one knew anything. Cargoes were always being moved in and out of the Queenstown docks and there was no special reason to take note of any particular one. No-one could be found who would admit to any knowledge of hired transport. When the customs office was visited by the constabulary, Seamus McBride was adamant that the cargo was clean. It was not until later in the day that word came through to Haulbowline Island from the Admiralty that it was now known that Customs and Excise in London had despatched a warning cable to Queenstown before the arrival of the *Taronga Park*; but when the police went in to question McBride again, McBride, having seen the red light, had gone to ground. His confidence that a simple denial of receipt would be believed had evaporated.

The trail was dead. Gun-running was now considered a possibility. A number of suspects, those known to have sympathies with the patriot cause, were arrested and questioned. Nothing emerged at all. In every part of Ireland police and troop dispositions were made; but the word went by the grapevine ahead of them and they met a blank wall.

* * *

Halfhyde and the rest were all free now: the glowing ember of turf had done its work. Halfhyde was all ready to push on into Connemara. That, according to the conversation overheard in the wagon train, was where Higgins was heading with his consignment of arms.

Foster said dubiously, 'There's the bog, sir. No guide now.'

'We shall manage. We shall find the firm ground, never fear – it's daylight now and we'll be able to see and feel our way well enough, perhaps with O'Dowd's help.' He put a hand on the old seaman's shoulder. 'You, O'Dowd. I think you know Connemara?'

'I do, sir,' O'Dowd said.

'Then you'll be a godsend. Have you experience of the bogs as well?'

O'Dowd said he had.

'Good! Then you shall lead us.' Halfhyde lifted an eyebrow as Foster stepped forward again. 'Yes, Mr Foster, what is it?'

'I take it you'll alert the authorities, sir—'

'Then you take it wrong, Mr Foster. I have a personal score to settle with Porteous Higgins – Gaboon too. I think we all have – and also, remember the girl's in danger if the authorities should blunder in, and blundering is a habit of authority. Now – no more delay.'

They started off. Leaving the cabin they followed O'Dowd, who seemed to know by some inbred Irish instinct exactly where they had reached firm ground on their arrival. They went out across the bog, keeping as before in single file, close behind O'Dowd. The old man took it slow, stepping cautiously, feeling to right and left at every step before going on. Soon they began to distinguish the difference in the look of the firm ground as opposed to the morass. O'Dowd said it was easy enough in the daytime, and soon he was making more speed as his confidence grew. After they had been moving along for a little more than an hour, they had a stroke of gruesome luck.

Ahead of them Halfhyde had spotted some disturbance in the bog, not far off the track. There were curious bubblings as though air was trying to escape, and the surface seemed to be heaving, and as they slowed and watched in awe something broke the bog's surface, something was thrust grotesquely up like the roll of a whale in the Great Australian Bight and then an arm was revealed by the bog's action, an arm that appeared to be waving them on.

The hand was clutching something in a death grip: a revolver. Halfhyde went forward, knelt on one knee, and reached out. As he strained towards the hand, two men laid hold of his legs and, safely held, he let his body go out over the bog. The stench filled his nostrils. The dead man must be from the party that had imprisoned them in the cabin, come to grief on the return journey to the Lord knew where . . . Halfhyde went to the limit of his reach and found that his fingers just touched the revolver. Another push and he found himself lying almost on the stinking surface. He got a grip of the gun but found he was quite unable to remove it from the dead fingers.

'We'll have to pull him clear,' he said breathlessly. 'Once on firm ground . . .'

He took hold of the arm behind the wrist, using both his hands. Foster and the others pulled, using Halfhyde's body as a makeshift tow-rope. Gradually they overcame the suction of the bog; the body rose, its face ghastly, the features still contorted in utter terror, set into the grimace of a horrible end. They pulled it half-way clear so that the torso was on the firm pathway, the legs still gripped by the marsh. Halfhyde forced the fingers apart and removed the revolver. He checked the chambers: they were all loaded. After being cleaned, it should be serviceable. He felt rising excitement and a grim determination to get Porteous Higgins in his sights.

They let the body go and it sank back with a gurgling sound, sliding down into the ooze, leaving a dip in the surface until the mud filled it again and left no trace behind.

SIXTEEN

It was a long way to Connemara: from Queenstown to Galway City was a distance of around a hundred miles. Halfhyde said, 'I estimate we're currently some twenty miles from Queenstown, and nor'-west of it.' A word earlier with O'Dowd had established that they were in the vicinity of the Boggeragh Mountains. 'We'll not go all the way by road, I think. I take it there'll not be much transport on the roads to give us lifts?'

He had addressed O'Dowd. The old seaman said, 'Little enough, sir, and that not going far.' Halfhyde nodded thoughtfully; the country districts of Ireland were poor enough in the main. There would be the odd big house that would hold carriage people and might have a conveyance abroad, but mostly the people would be labourers on the farms or peasants who eked out a mean living on their own couple of acres, not the sort of people to possess personal transport other than a donkey.

Halfhyde pulled a small compass from his pocket and gave O'Dowd a quizzical look. He asked, 'How far from here, d'you think, to the Kenmare River?'

'The Kenmare River, sir? Why, it'd be perhaps . . . twenty miles, sir. Maybe less.'

'And the bearing?'

O'Dowd scratched his head. 'Nor'-westerly, sir—'

'As I thought. And there'll be fishing boats. How would you rate their availability, O'Dowd?'

'You mean charter one, sir, or—'

'Beg, borrow or steal – and the latter would be the safest,

167

since to trust is not easy in these parts. Well, gentlemen, we're seamen and we should act as such. The devil take a trudge over fields and bogs and mountains! We make for Kenmare – at our best possible speed.'

* * *

The person Casey had referred to as 'the man' had not yet come; Higgins' temper grew foul as the days passed. He was anxious to get his hands on his payment, anxious to be away again to Australia and his business concerns. He was impatient with the necessity of keeping under cover, of having his free movement restricted. But as Casey said, though few enough people would be around to see him, discretion was important just the same. Sometimes, Casey said, a constable came along on his bicycle – just a routine call, but if Higgins was seen there would be questions. Strangers were a rarity in Connemara and by this time the *Taronga Park* would have come under suspicion.

'Queenstown's a long way south,' Higgins said sourly.

'True. Just so long as you covered your tracks well. And, of course, the British won't know what was in the cargo. But there's still a need for caution.'

'How long is this man going to be?'

Casey shrugged. 'Ach, there's no knowing. He's a law to himself, is the man. And he has a lot of ground to cover.' He added, 'He may not come here. You may need to go to him if he thinks it unwise to show himself openly.'

'I'll go to no-one,' Higgins said.

Casey laughed. 'If you want your money, you'll go and look pleased about it. The man . . . he's too important to be risked. I'm not saying he'll not come, but he may send word for you to Tuam or Galway City even.'

Angrily Higgins paced the floor of the cottage. He was anxious to be away now; every moment held possible danger to himself and the sooner he could reach England and a ship back to Sydney, the better. He could assist Ireland just as well from there, indeed to more effect. With luck, there would be more arms shipments, a very profitable way of patriotism. If only the man would come; Casey had gone on to stress the man's importance without being too precise and Higgins, making a guess, believed he could be the biggest of the Irish republicans, even such names as Thomas Clarke and James Connolly coming to mind. If the man were one of that band, then it was understandable that he would keep in the background.

The day passed, slowly. Casey's black-clad mother still sat by the turf fire, muttering and chewing, her sunken lips and cheeks moving in and out but her body otherwise motionless as though she were already dead. Victoria Penn prepared a meal of many potatoes and a little meat. Gaboon sat on the other side of the fire from the old woman, watchful and as ever silent. As the evening shadows fell a dreary drizzle started and Casey came in from the yard to say that the constable was approaching, head down against the rain, his blue cloak streaming water.

'I'll keep him outside,' Casey said. 'Be very quiet now.'

They were. Higgins had his revolver ready. The constable had a narrow escape. When he had bicycled away Casey came back. The constable had been enquiring after strangers. Naturally, Casey had seen none.

'Didn't he want to look in here?' Higgins asked.

'I am trusted by the law,' Casey answered.

The rest of that night and the next day passed without incident; but after the dark had come down once again there was another visitor. Casey looking from the window, saw a swaying lantern coming along the rough track to the cottage. Once again he went outside, cautioning the others to silence. When he came back he had a young man with him, soaking wet and travel-stained. Too young, surely, to be one of the big names?

Seeing the enquiry in Higgins' eye, Casey said, 'This is not the man. Not yet. And the man'll not come here. Our friend is to take you to him at once, in Galway City.'

* * *

It had been another long trek for Halfhyde. A little after midnight of the day O'Dowd had led them through the bog to safety, the seamen had dropped down upon the river estuary and were walking into Kenmare on the northern bank. Halfhyde halted the party in the lee of a warehouse by the riverside, looking for a suitable vessel.

He could take his choice.

There were plenty of fishing-boats, lying quietly alongside the quay. Most of them, O'Dowd said, if not all of them, would be deserted while the fishermen slept in their homes ashore. Halfhyde had thought as much. He said, 'We'll take the one furthest to seaward. All ready, Mr Foster?'

'All ready, sir.'

'Bear off the moment we're aboard, then, and get the sails on her. There's enough wind to carry us past Lambs Head. Quickly, now!'

They moved down fast for the quay, shadows in the night, and clambered aboard in as much silence as was possible; while the hands cast off the ropes and then bore away, giving the boat a hard thrust out into the stream, Halfhyde and Foster started to haul up the canvas. As the mains'l was hoisted to the masthead the wind took it, billowing it out, and Halfhyde ran for the wheel in the sternsheets. Within little more than five minutes after they had boarded, the fishing-boat was nicely under way and heading before a fair wind down the estuary to the open sea. When they reached Lambs Head Halfhyde would turn for the north, past Ballinskelligs Bay and Bolus Head, making up for Great Blasket Island and then on for the port of Galway. Once again Foster had been doubtful about Halfhyde's proposals; but Halfhyde had been adamant that so far as possible he was going to deal with Higgins and Gaboon himself, only calling in the police and military as a last resort.

'I have an idea Higgins can be flushed into the open,' he said, 'without assistance from the authorities.'

'But how, sir?'

'I shall find a way of making ourselves obvious, Mr Foster – no beating about the bush – you'll see!'

He would say no more than that. Now, moving to seaward down the Kenmare River, he was content to be back in his own element and once again in command afloat, however small the vessel might be. He could see that the others were equally pleased; none of them had much love for the land or the business of ploughing across open country. Night-shrouded, with no lights visible anywhere, that country sped past on either hand. Halfhyde was feeling the thrill of the chase as the boat surged forward. Higgins was going to be most mightily surprised; scared, too. And a man both surprised and scared was apt to do foolish things.

Halfhyde cast a prayer into the wind: a prayer that God might assist him in scattering Higgins' wits at an appropriate moment. Higgins had had a good start, but his advantage was lessening by the minute. As they came out of the estuary past Lambs Head they met a heavier wind from the south-west and began dipping and plunging as Halfhyde hauled round to the north.

* * *

For Higgins, accompanied by Gaboon and Victoria – he had refused point-blank to leave them behind – it was a long and gruelling walk into Galway City along a rutted apology for a road, in darkness that was scarcely dispelled by the candle flame in the lantern carried by the young guide. There was rain, blown into their faces by an increasing wind; and where the track was not stony it was soon a sheet of mud. Every now and again the lantern blew out, and had to be re-lit, a difficult task in the blustering wind. There was no moon, no stars; heavy cloud lay over all. Higgins cursed viciously in a low monotone of discontent. Gaboon trudged along with his head down, issuing animal noises of discomfort and tiredness but keeping immediately behind the girl. Once another lantern was seen ahead, and the young man immediately doused his own candle and led the party off the track to lie low in a field where turf had been cut deep. They lay beneath the surface level, in a sludgy pool of water until the lantern-bearer had gone past, singing in a drunken voice, happy enough until the fumes of whiskey evaporated to leave him with his alcoholic remorse and a drumming head. Nearer the town the guide led them across country, skirting the southern shore of Lough Corrib to join the road leading down from Oughterard, the road upon which

171

Higgins' father had been taken by the English soldiers. They came at last into the outskirts of Galway, crossed the bridge over the water, Lough Corrib's drain into Galway Bay, passed Queen's College, moved on through a maze of alleys until they emerged into the main street by Alexander Moon's drapery shop, and thence continued westerly until they entered the Claddagh with its largely Spanish architecture and its population of fishermen, a place of quays and a smell of fish, and small hovels now dark and silent.

There was no sign of life at all. Higgins and the others were the only moving things.

They followed their guide into a narrow alley and then beneath an archway into a small littered courtyard that could have come from any Spanish town. Higgins knew the history of Galway well enough: on the wild, rock-girt coasts of Ireland's west many of the great ships of the Armada had been driven ashore after fleeing northwards from the English fleet, all the way from the Channel, around the north of Scotland via Duncansby Head and Cape Wrath to spill their men in the Irish storms. Many had lived through it and had been cast ashore, and their influence had remained in the style of the Claddagh buildings and in the dark-eyed people of the west.

The young man stopped at a door at the far side of the yard. He knocked: three taps in quick succession, then two at spaced intervals.

The door was opened almost at once; darkness yawned. A voice said, 'Come in. Take care, now.' There was no light; they all crowded in and the door was shut and bolted behind them. The man who had opened the door pushed through towards the back. After a pause another door opened and light came through, yellow light that flickered off walls that had once been white-washed, off a low, dirty ceiling. The floor was bare stone, worn and smooth. The man with the lantern gestured them to go through a door to the left, into the room where the light came from.

Higgins went in first. There was a table with chairs set around it, four of them occupied. Higgins recognized three of the men: Seamus McBride from Queenstown was one. Two

172

others were from the group of men and women who had brought food to the wagons in the south. The fourth was not known to Higgins, but he assumed him to be the one he was to meet, the one referred to as the man, without a name. There was leadership about him: it lay in his eyes, which blazed with an inner fervour, a dedication, almost a mania. He was slimly built but tall, with a long, dark jaw, a long upper lip above it, and sunken cheeks that gave emphasis to the jaw and nose. And he looked dangerous. He smiled briefly at Higgins and said, 'So you've come. I'm sorry for the necessity, but it was the only safe way.' He paused. 'We're all very grateful for what you've brought, Mr Higgins.'

'I was pleased to do it,' Higgins said. He added, 'Whatever the risks – and they were many.'

The man shrugged, keeping his gaze on Higgins. 'There were risks indeed. But the son of Hannibal Higgins would not take too much thought for the risks – would he now?'

There was something in the tone that Higgins didn't care for. He said, 'No, he would not—'

'And he would be generous in the cause of Ireland – would he not?'

Higgins licked at his lips, finding them suddenly dry. He glanced aside at Gaboon. Gaboon, the hairy face in shadow, was motionless, seeming mesmerized by the eyes of the man at the table. Higgins said, 'I've never been ungenerous. I'm not quite sure what you mean. I'm sure you know I've come for payment for the arms?'

The man nodded, a slight smile on his face again. 'Yes, this I know. But I have something to say, Mr Higgins, and 'tis this.' He leaned forward, the eyes appearing even brighter now. 'We need money as well as arms. Our men are largely poor and though eager to fight must also live. It costs money also to send our patriots across to England and then to maintain them there until we're ready – you know what for. Money, Mr Higgins, is our life's blood, as much as arms.'

Higgins' eyes narrowed: he didn't like the atmosphere at all now. He said, 'You're asking for a donation. Is that it?'

'That's the substance of it, yes. Are you willing to make it,

Mr Higgins?'

Higgins said, 'I don't know. My money's in Australia. It would take time. But once I'm back, I could make the necessary arrangements, I don't doubt.'

'That's true. But once you were back there, Mr Higgins . . . and in the meantime there's the question of payment for the arms you've brought. 'Tis not easy for us to raise the cash. As a patriot, I believe you'll not be pressing us.'

'I have to live too,' Higgins said. 'If I'm not paid for the present consignment, I shall have no cash to buy arms for you in the future.' He paused, eyes watchful. 'There could have been many more cargoes.'

The man said calmly, 'There *will* be many more. You will go back to Australia and arrange for more shipments whenever we have a need in the future. If you do not . . .' The voice had become very hard. 'If you do not, then certain information will be laid both here and in Australia, and you will find yourself hanged for treason.'

Higgins stood very still. His face was white. He could scarcely believe what he was hearing. It had knocked him sideways; but he forced himself to take it easy: he held the whip hand still. 'There is no evidence,' he said. 'You're full of blarney. McBride'll never inform against me, or he'll hang too when the English arrest him, which they would, even if I—'

'Wait,' the man said, holding up a hand. 'You forget someone else, I think.'

'Who?'

'Captain Halfhyde.'

There was a silence. Higgins looked in a state of shock. Breaking the silence he said hoarsely, 'Halfhyde's dead.'

The man shook his head. 'He is not dead. Your orders were not carried out. Halfhyde lives and is in our hands – so are his crew, those whom you brought with you from the ship. They will be produced whenever I give the word.' He glanced at the patriots from the southern bog. One of them confirmed that the men from the *Taronga Park* were alive. They were, he told Higgins, being held in County Kerry. Higgins' body began to shake. Gaboon took a pace forward, shoulders hunched, long arms held out in front. Both he and Higgins knew that six witnesses would be ready to testify to murder on the high seas if what the man had said was true. Higgins, in fact, was not convinced. He didn't believe the bog-dwellers from the south would be likely to take the risk of letting the prisoners live.

He pulled out his revolver.

* * *

It had been Halfhyde's misfortune to meet an adverse shift of wind soon after he had hauled away to the north from the Kenmare River; his made-good distance had been sadly little and it was some thirty-six hours after his purloining of the fishing-boat that he raised the Aran Islands at the entrance to Galway Bay. Dusk was coming down as, with some forty miles yet to go, he took the boat up towards the South Sound to leave Inishmaan on his port side. From here he met a more favourable wind, the blustery wind that had blown into the face of Higgins on his journey towards Galway; even so, it was full dark by the time he had come alongside the quay in the fishing port. Full dark, but the bars were open, light filtered from the windows behind the grocers' shops and from the doors the occasional drunks emerged.

'Now, Mr Foster,' Halfhyde said as he led the way over the bulwarks. 'We shall buy ourselves a drink or two. I think we've earned it! And at the same time we shall advertise our presence.'

They trooped into the nearest bar and Halfhyde ordered whiskies, putting down his money with a peremptory air. The proprietor looked at the coins.

'' 'Tis not real money,' he said indignantly.

'It's real enough, my friend, but it's Australian currency, and all I have to spend.'

'There'll be no whisky for it,' the grocer said with an air of finality. 'You'll get nothing here without English money.'

'English?' Halfhyde said loudly. He spoke with arrogance. 'I fancied you Irish had no love for England, yet you insist upon English money—'

'We have not the choice.'

'And just as well, I say.' Behind Halfhyde a silence had fallen on the bar. Enmity could be felt like a knife in the back, but Halfhyde kept his gaze on the proprietor. He went on, still loudly, 'I have come from Australia to find a man who may be known to you. His name is Higgins . . . Porteous Higgins.'

The silence could be felt even more. The grocer asked, 'And yours?'

'St Vincent Halfhyde, a lieutenant of Her Majesty's Navy,' he answered, twisting the truth a little. He turned sharply, ran his gaze over the dark faces huddled together on a bench. 'Does anyone here know Porteous Higgins, and his present whereabouts?'

There was no answer. The hostile faces stared back at Halfhyde. Maybe they had heard of Higgins, maybe they hadn't; but they had taken the point that here before them stood men who had no time for Irish patriots, men apparently of the Queen's service who meant harm to republicanism and the Clan-na-Gael. Halfhyde stared them out contemptuously for a while longer, then turned on his heel. 'Come,' he said to his companions. 'We'll not stay where there is no drink and no welcome.'

He strode to the door, followed by Foster and the others. Out in the street again he said in a low voice, 'We've set the cat among the pigeons with a vengeance, Mr Foster.'

Foster said, 'It'll just act as a warning, sir!'

Halfhyde gave a short laugh. 'Not entirely so. In Kenmare I spoke of doing something to make us obvious, did I not? We are now the magnet, Mr Foster – the magnet that will attract the patriots of whom there must be a cell in Galway City or I'm a Dutchman. And where you find the cell, you find the way to Porteous Higgins! All we need to do is wait – and keep alert, and outsmart them.'

He felt in his pocket for the revolver brought from the bog, now cleaned and fully serviceable. Six bullets that would need to be enough to stand between his life and the Clan-na-Gael.

SEVENTEEN

The knock, the signal as used earlier by the guide who had come to Casey's cottage, had come at the very moment that Higgins had drawn his revolver. As he swung round involuntarily Seamus McBride moved fast and grabbed his arm. The steely grip around his wrist made Higgins drop the revolver. McBride bent and picked it up.

'All right now,' he said, his eyes hard. 'There'll be no more of that, either from you or the dumb one.'

Higgins' gaze darted from left to right and back again; he had a hunted look now. Gaboon was mouthing something; the girl, standing back by the door, was white and scared. From outside in the passage they heard the bolts being withdrawn; then the door shut and a moment later the doorkeeper came into the room with another man, a man in a state of agitation. He spoke rapidly to the tall man, the leader, who had still not been named. Higgins was unable to follow what he said; he appeared to be speaking in Gaelic. But Higgins caught two names unmistakably: one was his own, the other Halfhyde's. When his own name was mentioned, the man gave him a hard look before turning his attention back to the new arrival.

Then he said, 'Halfhyde is here in Galway City. Got clear away . . . he is looking for you, Higgins. He'll not be finding you. We leave at once.'

'For Tuam?'

'Not for Tuam. There are plenty of other places we can go to. If Halfhyde comes here, he'll find no evidence of any of us.' The man paused, staring at Higgins. 'From now on, you'll obey my orders if you wish to live.'

* * *

Halfhyde and his party had gone to ground before the messenger had left the bar. Not far away, down by the quay, was a pile of disused gear – old fishing nets, worn-out rope fenders, pieces of timber. The quay area was in thick darkness; they were soon concealed. There was a long wait before the door of the bar opened and, in the light coming from behind, a man could be seen, looking to right and left before emerging. Then the door shut and footsteps were heard, breaking an eerie silence. As they began to fade Halfhyde got to his feet. He removed his boots.

'I shall follow,' he said to Foster. 'The rest of you wait here. I may be led to someone who knows where Higgins is, or I may not. In either case I shall be back when I've seen where the man goes.'

He moved away at a crouch from the heap of junk, slipping shadow-like across the cobbles, making for the lee of a warehouse that stood on a street corner opposite the grocer's shop. He could hear the footsteps ahead, moving fast now. Keeping close to the low buildings he began to make out the shape of his quarry, a darker outline than the night itself. In his stockinged feet he went ahead silently, the revolver ready in his hand. As it happened he had not far to go. He followed the sound of the feet into an alley leading off the street to the left, then caught a sight of the dark blur moving beneath an archway. As the man disappeared his footsteps could still be heard. Halfhyde moved on cautiously, flattened himself against the side of the arch and peered round. Now he could see little; just the vague shape of buildings forming a hollow square. Then he heard the knock at the door, loud, with a suggestion of panic urgency. Three quick taps in succession, then a pause; Another knock, then after an interval another – a pre-arranged signal.

Now there was no time to be lost. Halfhyde turned back along the alley to fetch Foster and the rest of his party. As he did so he became aware of a shadow moving towards him, fast; so fast that he had no chance. A heavy man came for him head down, butting him hard in the stomach, and he went down gasping, winded and writhing on the cobbles. He was aware of something being lifted over him, a heavy object that looked like a club, a shillelagh. He managed to swivel his body as the club came down, and it hit into the cobbles with tremendous force, force that must have sent agonizing shivers up the man's arm. There was a vicious curse, and then Halfhyde had a grip on a leg and was heaving with all his strength. The man went down forcefully on one shoulder. Back on his feet now, Halfhyde bent and dragged him up, thrusting the heavy body back hard against a wall behind. As he did so he heard footsteps from the direction of the arch, and he looked round. Five or six shadows, he believed, heading the other way from inside the arch. Before Halfhyde could stop him with a hand around his throat, the man shouted a warning and the footsteps stopped. There was a pause, then Halfhyde fancied he heard stealthy movement coming towards him from the direction of the archway. His revolver was somewhere on the ground, torn from his hand when he was butted in the stomach.

Swinging his prisoner across his body as a shield, he waited, his heart thudding. The warning shout hadn't aroused anyone from the hovels: in Galway City those not involved in clandestine matters kept themselves out of trouble, remained in the safety of their beds. Beyond the approaching men, Half-hyde made out a bulkier shadow that he believed could be Porteous Higgins.

Now the moving men were very close. Halfhyde waited until the last moment, then he went into sudden action. He hurled his prisoner straight into the first man to move up, then went for the next, landing a heavy blow to the face. He felt the crunch of bone; there was a cry and the man fell. From ahead a revolver opened fire and Halfhyde felt the close wind of a bullet. As another man came for him he dodged aside, thrusting out one of his stockinged feet, and the man went headlong, howling as his face hit the cobbles.

Then there was a commotion in the rear, the sound of running feet and an assortment of shouts. Halfhyde caught the

179

Irish tones of old O'Dowd's voice raised high, yelling blue murder at would-be rebels. Foster must have heard that warning shout and now his sudden advent was causing consternation to the patriots.

Something was happening ahead: the shadows were on the move, and there was more gunfire as two of them appeared briefly on the roof of one of the hovels. Ahead of his party, Halfhyde ran forward to a corner where two alleys crossed. Alongside a wall was a large water-butt and a drainpipe; on the roof, clambering to drop down the other side, were Higgins and Gaboon, scrambling shakily on the slates, a desperate effort to get away from two sets of hostile men. As Halfhyde came up, a revolver opened fire again: one of the escaping patriots, emptying a whole six chambers into the figures silhouetted against the night sky.

* * *

The Royal Irish Constabulary had arrived, a little late. Higgins and Gaboon had slid helplessly down the roof and now lay in grotesque attitudes on the cobbles. Gaboon was dead; Higgins lived yet. He would be made to talk. Victoria and Halfhyde stood together; the girl was weeping and shivering uncontrollably. Halfhyde comforted her. A sergeant of the RIC came back from ahead as he held the girl in his arms.

'They've flown,' he said.

'What chance of picking them up?'

The sergeant shrugged. 'Little enough indeed. They have too many places, too many people who'll give them shelter.' He paused, looking Halfhyde up and down in the light of a police lantern. 'Now, sir: you sound like a gentleman, and an English one at that. May I ask what your involvement is?'

'You may indeed.' Halfhyde told him the story as briefly as he could. He indicated Higgins and Gaboon. 'These two are the arms purveyors,' he said. 'Arms for the Clan-na-Gael or whatever they call themselves these days. Sinn Fein, perhaps—I don't know.'

'So it was arms for certain, was it?' the sergeant asked.

'You know about it?'

'I do. There was a warning . . . but it was not specifically about arms. I think the nature of the cargo was not positively known—'

'But they did know it was suspect?'

'They did, sir.'

So had Perry got through after all? If so he was owed a very large debt. Halfhyde, with his past experience of the Admiralty, had a strong suspicion that official delays and pomposity on the part of men in senior positions had nearly cost him his life. He said, 'I'm hopeful Higgins will talk about where those arms have gone. I suggest he's given medical attention as soon as possible.'

The sergeant said he would see to that. He moved away, giving orders. Halfhyde waited until Higgins had been removed in a police ambulance, the iron-shod wheels rumbling away over the cobbles behind the horse. Then he accompanied the sergeant to the police barracks; telephone conversations, carried out at length with Haulbowline Island, where Captain Warrender was brought from his bed, confirmed Halfhyde's *bona fides*. The party and the girl were provided with hotel accommodation for the night, and next morning they took the train to Athenry where they changed for Queenstown. Upon arrival they were taken to the Naval base where Captain Warrender was waiting to talk to Halfhyde.

'Well done,' he said. 'You've played your part nobly, my dear fellow. You can leave the rest to us.'

'To be settled quickly, I hope. I have a ship to worry about. I trust she'll not be impounded?'

'Oh, by no means. Of course there's the question of the tow, of a claim for salvage. A damn long tow if I may say so! And mightily expensive.'

Halfhyde said gloomily, 'Expensive to the point of my bankrupcty, I fear.'

'No, no. Not necessarily. You've done the country some service after all, Halfhyde. The authorities may be persuaded to help – who knows?'

Who knows indeed, Halfhyde thought, still gloomy, as he made his way across the harbour in a Naval picquet-boat half an hour later. The authorities, Naval or otherwise, had never been disposed towards generosity. However, the *Taronga Park* was safe and seaworthy, or would be once an engine repair – another expensive item – had been made; and that was something on the credit side. On the debit side was poor Perry, now announced by Warrender to have died in Santiago. In the course of his duty . . . Perry had been a very good man.

And the girl, seated alongside him in the sternsheets and looking perky again and hopeful?

What of her?

Halfhyde suspected he was landed with her and knew not whether to be sorry or pleased. He travelled the fastest who travelled alone . . . One person who would not be pleased was Vice-Admiral Sir John Willard. It would be seen as most distasteful by Lady Willard, an insult to Mildred. And Sir John would be catching the backlash of her tongue.